PRAISE FOR *BAREE*

"Cliffhanging adventures abound for Baree through the course of the story, and Curwood's natural story-telling abilities coupled with his knowledge of the wilderness makes them realistic and believable. This is an exciting, colorful tale that...ranks with the work of Jack London."

—*Voice of Youth Advocates (VOYA)*

"Baree becomes accidently separated from his parents before he's quite out of puppyhood. He learns to fend for himself the hard way, a life that is particularly difficult....In the end he finds his home with humans. Curwood writes in a straightforward style that captures the simplicity and beauty of nature."

—*ALA Booklist*

"Baree's dramatic coming of age entails such key moments as letting out his first wolf howl; realizing that there are creatures more powerful than he in the wild; and having a pack of wolves turn on him....A sensitively written novel—about life in the wild and especially about how animals may perceive experiences—that's bound to find fans."

—*Kirkus Reviews*

BAREE

THE STORY OF A WOLF-DOG

BAREE

THE STORY OF A WOLF-DOG

Originally published as
Baree, Son of Kazan

JAMES OLIVER CURWOOD

NEWMARKET PRESS NEW YORK

Baree, Son of Kazan copyright 1917 by James Oliver Curwood
Copyright renewed 1944 by Ethel M. Curwood
Expanded edition of *Baree, The Story of a Wolf-Dog*
copyright © 1990 by Newmarket Press

The original text of *Baree, Son of Kazan* has been
updated to reflect current spelling usage.

Photograph on page 6 by Jim Brandenburg.

This book published simultaneously in
the United States of America and in Canada.

10   9   8   7   6

Library of Congress Cataloging-in-Publication Data
Curwood, James Oliver, 1878–1927.
[Baree, son of Kazan]
Baree, the story of a wolf-dog / James Oliver Curwood.
p.   cm.
Reprint. Originally published: Baree, son of Kazan.
Garden City, N.Y.: Doubleday, Page, 1917.
ISBN 1-55704-075-3 (hard)
ISBN 1-55704-132-6 (Medallion pbk)
1. Dogs—Fiction.   2. Wolves—Fiction.   I. Title
PS3505.U92B32   1990
813'.52—dc20   90-37875
                                         CIP

QUANTITY PURCHASES

Companies, professional groups, clubs, and other organizations
may qualify for special terms when ordering quantities of this title.
For information contact: Special Sales, Newmarket Press,
18 East 48th Street, New York, N.Y. 10017, or call (212) 832-3575.

Book design by M. J. DiMassi
Manufactued in the United States of America

PUBLISHER'S NOTE

The wonderful movie *The Bear*, released in America in 1989, first made us aware of the Michigan adventure and nature author James Oliver Curwood. His 1916 novel *The Grizzly King* was the inspiration for Jean-Jacques Annaud's award-winning film about the escape of an orphaned cub and a giant grizzly from two hunters. Back in bookstores and on library shelves 73 years after it was first published, *The Bear* (as we retitled our new Newmarket edition) won rave reviews from critics and readers alike, effectively creating a new James Oliver Curwood "fan club," of which we're proud to be charter members.

I can now happily recommend another wonderful Curwood novel, *Baree, The Story of a Wolf-Dog* (which was originally published in 1917 under the title of *Baree, Son of Kazan*). I am delighted to report that we believe this too is a long-lost classic, the third book in what Curwood called his "Nature Series."

Curwood writes in his preface to *Baree* that he hopes his "animal books" will teach us a little of what he himself learned about wild life. "If we are to love wild animals so much that we do not want to kill them we *must know them as they actually live.*" And so a year after creating Muskwa, the unforgettable bear cub, Curwood takes us into the world of Baree, the son of a wolf-dog named Kazan and of a blind full-blooded wolf named Gray Wolf.

Baree will become as memorable to you as *The Bear*. It will further acquaint a new generation of readers to the writing—and the message—of one of America's outstanding spokespersons for conservation and ecology. Curwood writes with authority from his true experiences in the wilds. He also demonstrates that he is a grand storyteller, and we're sure you will enjoy the adventures of his Baree.

ESTHER MARGOLIS,
President and Publisher,
Newmarket Press, New York City
Spring, 1992

PREFACE

SINCE the publication of my two animal books, "Kazan" and "The Grizzly King,"[1] I have received so many hundreds of letters from friends of wild animal life, all of which were more or less of an enquiring nature, that I have been encouraged to incorporate in this preface of the third of my series—"Baree, Son of Kazan"[2]—something more of my desire and hope of writing of wild life, and something of the foundation of fact whereupon this and its companion books have been written.

I have always disliked the preaching of sermons in the pages of romance. It is like placing a halter about an unsuspecting reader's neck and dragging him into paths for which he may have no liking. But if fact and truth produce in the reader's mind a message for himself, then a work has been done. That is what I hope for in my nature books. The American people are not and never have been lovers of wild life. As a nation we have gone after Nature with a gun.

[1]Retitled *The Bear—A Novel* in the 1989 Newmarket edition.
[2]Retitled *Baree, The Story of a Wolf-Dog* in this Newmarket edition.

And what right, you may ask, has a confessed slaughterer of wildlife such as I have been to complain? None at all, I assure you. I have twenty-seven guns—and I have used them all. I stand condemned as having done more than my share toward extermination. But that does not lessen the fact that I have learned; and in learning I have come to believe that if boys and girls and men and women could be brought into the homes and lives of wild birds and animals as their homes are made and their lives are lived we would all understand at last that wherever a heart beats it is very much like our own in the final analysis of things. To see a bird singing on a twig means but little; but to live a season with that bird, to be with it in courting days, in matehood and motherhood, to understand its griefs as well as its gladness means a great deal. And in my books it is my desire to tell of the lives of the wild things which I know as they are actually lived. It is not my desire to humanize them. If we are to love wild animals so much that we do not want to kill them we *must know them as they actually live.* And in their lives, in the *facts* of their lives, there is so much of real and honest romance and tragedy, so much that makes them akin to ourselves that the animal biographer need not step aside from the paths of actuality to hold one's interest.

Perhaps rather tediously I have come to the few words I want to say about Baree, the hero of this book. Baree, after all, is only another Kazan. For it was Kazan I found in the way I have described—a bad dog, a killer about to be shot to death by his master when chance, and my own faith in him, gave him to me.

We traveled together for many thousands of miles through the northland—on trails to the Barren Lands, to Hudson's Bay and to the Arctic. Kazan, the bad dog, the half-wolf, the killer—was the best four-legged friend I ever had. He died near Fort MacPherson, on the Peel River, and is buried there. And Kazan was the father of Baree; Gray Wolf, the full-blooded wolf was his mother. Nepeese, The Willow, still lives near God's Lake; and it was in the country of Nepeese and her father that for three lazy months I watched the doings at Beaver Town, and went on fishing trips with Wakayoo, the bear. Sometimes I have wondered if old Beaver-tooth himself did not in some way understand that I had made his colony safe for his people. It was Pierrot's trapping ground; and to Pierrot—father of Nepeese—I gave my best rifle on his word that he would not harm my beaver friends for two years. And the people of Pierrot's breed keep their word. Wakayoo, Baree's big bear friend, is dead. He was killed as I have described, in that "pocket" among the ridges, while I was on a jaunt to Beaver Town. We were becoming good friends and I missed him a great deal. The story of Pierrot and of his princess wife, Wyola, is true; they are buried side by side under the tall spruce that stood near their cabin. Pierrot's murderer, instead of dying as I have told it, was killed in his attempt to escape the Royal Mounted farther west. When I last saw Baree he was at Lac Seul House, where I was the guest of Mr. William Patterson, the factor; and the last word I heard from him was through my good friend Frank

Aldous, factor at White Dog Post, who wrote me only a few weeks ago that he had recently seen Nepeese and Baree and the husband of Nepeese, and that the happiness he found in their far wilderness home made him regret that he was a bachelor. I feel sorry for Aldous. He is a splendid young Englishman, unattached, and someday I am going to try and marry him off. I have in mind someone at the present moment— a fox-trapper's daughter up near the Barren, very pretty, and educated at a Missioner's school; and as Aldous is going with me on my next trip I may have something to say about them in the book that is to follow "Baree, Son of Kazan."

—JAMES OLIVER CURWOOD
Owosso, Michigan
June 12, 1917

BAREE

THE STORY OF A WOLF-DOG

the appearance of [illegible]. The remaining hours
would be spent [illegible] to eat, play, all the while
interacting, and most important, itself the pack unity.
Wintertime [illegible] was the stark contrast and more
and the year changed again, structure to the pack. The
world began [illegible] their young. Before giving birth
they would [illegible]. The [illegible] of the family unit
had been cast into [illegible] as it had. This month now
on, the activities with each sparring endeavors
that favored rescue dependant during times of the

CHAPTER I

TO Baree, for many days after he was born, the world was a vast gloomy cavern.

During these first days of his life his home was in the heart of a great windfall where Gray Wolf, his blind mother, had found a safe nest for his babyhood, and to which Kazan, her mate, came only now and then, his eyes gleaming like strange balls of greenish fire in the darkness. It was Kazan's eyes that gave to Baree his first impression of something existing away from his mother's side, and they brought to him also his discovery of vision. He could feel, he could smell, he could hear—but in that black pit under the fallen timber he had never *seen* until the eyes came. At first they frightened him; then they puzzled him, and his fear changed to an immense curiosity. He would be looking straight at them, when all at once they would disappear. This was when Kazan turned his head. And then they would flash back at him again out of the darkness with such startling suddenness that Baree would involuntarily shrink closer to his

7

mother, who always trembled and shivered in a strange way when Kazan came in.

Baree, of course, would never know their story. He would never know that Gray Wolf, his mother, was a full-blooded wolf, and that Kazan, his father, was a dog. In him nature was already beginning its wonderful work, but it would never go beyond certain limitations. It would tell him, in time, that his beautiful wolf-mother was blind, but he would never know of that terrible battle between Gray Wolf and the lynx in which his mother's sight had been destroyed. Nature could tell him nothing of Kazan's merciless vengeance, of the wonderful years of their matehood, of their loyalty, their strange adventures in the great Canadian wilderness—it could make him only a son of Kazan.

But at first, and for many days, it was all mother. Even after his eyes had opened wide and he had found his legs so that he could stumble about a little in the darkness, nothing existed for Baree but his mother. When he was old enough to be playing with sticks and moss out in the sunlight, he still did not know what she looked like. But to him she was big and soft and warm, and she licked his face with her tongue, and talked to him in a gentle, whimpering way that at last made him find his own voice in a faint, squeaky yap.

And then came that wonderful day when the greenish balls of fire that were Kazan's eyes came nearer and nearer, a little at a time, and very cautiously. Heretofore Gray Wolf had warned him back. To be alone

8

was the first law of her wild breed during mothering-time. A low snarl from her throat, and Kazan had always stopped. But on this day the snarl did not come. In Gray Wolf's throat it died away in a low, whimpering sound. A note of loneliness, of gladness, of a great yearning. "It is all right now," she was saying to Kazan; and Kazan—pausing for a moment to make sure—replied with an answering note deep in his throat.

Still slowly, as if not quite sure of what he would find, Kazan came to them, and Baree snuggled closer to his mother. He heard Kazan as he dropped down heavily on his belly close to Gray Wolf. He was unafraid—and mightily curious. And Kazan, too, was curious. He sniffed. In the gloom his ears were alert. After a little Baree began to move. An inch at a time he dragged himself away from Gray Wolf's side. Every muscle in her lithe body tensed. Again her wolf blood was warning her. There was danger for Baree. Her lips drew back, baring her fangs. Her throat trembled, but the note in it never came. Out of the darkness two yards away came a soft, puppyish whine, and the caressing sound of Kazan's tongue.

Baree had felt the thrill of his first great adventure. He had discovered his father.

This all happened in the third week of Baree's life. He was just eighteen days old when Gray Wolf allowed Kazan to make the acquaintance of his son. If it had not been for Gray Wolf's blindness and the memory of that day on the Sun Rock when the lynx had destroyed her eyes, she would have given birth to Baree in the open, and his legs would have been quite strong.

9

He would have known the sun and the moon and the stars; he would have realized what the thunder meant, and would have seen the lightning flashing in the sky. But as it was, there had been nothing for him to do in that black cavern under the windfall but stumble about a little in the darkness, and lick with his tiny red tongue the raw bones that were strewn about them. Many times he had been left alone. He had heard his mother come and go, and nearly always it had been in response to a yelp from Kazan that came to them like a distant echo. He had never felt a very strong desire to follow until this day when Kazan's big, cool tongue caressed his face. In those wonderful seconds nature was at work. His instinct was not quite born until then. And when Kazan went away, leaving them alone in darkness, Baree whimpered for him to come back, just as he had cried for his mother when now and then she had left him in response to her mate's call.

The sun was straight above the forest when, an hour or two after Kazan's visit, Gray Wolf slipped away. Between Baree's nest and the top of the windfall were forty feet of jammed and broken timber through which not a ray of light could break. This blackness did not frighten him, for he had yet to learn the meaning of light. Day, and not night, was to fill him with his first great terror. So quite fearlessly, with a yelp for his mother to wait for him, he began to follow. If Gray Wolf heard him, she paid no attention to his call, and the scrape of her claws on the dead timber died swiftly away.

This time Baree did not stop at the eight-inch log which had always shut in his world in that particular direction. He clambered to the top of it and rolled over on the other side. Beyond this was vast adventure, and he plunged into it courageously.

It took him a long time to make the first twenty yards. Then he came to a log worn smooth by the feet of Gray Wolf and Kazan, and stopping every few feet to send out a whimpering call for his mother, he made his way farther and farther along it. As he went, there grew slowly a curious change in this world of his. He had known nothing but blackness. And now this blackness seemed breaking itself up into strange shapes and shadows. Once he caught the flash of a fiery streak above him—a gleam of sunshine—and it startled him so that he flattened himself down upon the log and did not move for half a minute. Then he went on. An ermine squeaked under him. He heard the swift rustling of a squirrel's feet, and a curious *whut-whut-whut* that was not at all like any sound his mother had ever made. He was off the trail.

The log was no longer smooth, and it was leading him upward higher and higher into the tangle of the windfall, and was growing narrower every foot he progressed. He whined. His soft little nose sought vainly for the warm scent of his mother. The end came suddenly when he lost his balance and fell. He let out a piercing cry of terror as he felt himself slipping, and then plunged downward. He must have been high up in the windfall, for to Baree it was a tremendous fall. His soft little body thumped from log to log as he shot this way and that, and when at last he stopped, there was scarcely a breath left in him. But he stood up quickly on his four trembling legs—and blinked.

A new terror held Baree rooted there. In an instant the whole world had changed. It was a flood of sunlight. Everywhere he looked he could see strange things. But it was the sun that frightened him most. It was his first impression of fire, and it made his eyes smart. He would have slunk back into the friendly gloom of the windfall, but at this moment Gray Wolf came around the end of a great log, followed by Kazan. She muzzled Baree joyously, and Kazan in a most doglike fashion wagged his tail. This mark of the dog was to be a part of Baree. Half wolf, he would always wag his tail. He tried to wag it now. Perhaps Kazan saw the effort, for he emitted a muffled yelp of approbation as he sat back on his haunches.

Or he might have been saying to Gray Wolf:

"Well, we've got the little rascal out of that windfall at last, haven't we?"

For Baree it had been a great day. He had discovered his father—and the world.

CHAPTER II

AND it was a wonderful world—a world of vast silence, empty of everything but the creatures of the wild. The nearest Hudson's Bay post was a hundred miles away, and the first town of civilization was a straight three hundred to the south. Two years before, Tusoo, the Cree trapper, had called this his domain. It had come down to him, as was the law of the forests, through generations of forefathers; but Tusoo had been the last of his worn-out family; he had died of smallpox, and his wife and his children had died with him. Since then no human foot had taken up his trails. The lynx had multiplied. The moose and caribou had gone unhunted by man. The beaver had built their homes undisturbed. The tracks of the black bear were as thick as the tracks of the deer farther south. And where once the deadfalls and poison baits of Tusoo had kept the wolves thinned down, there was no longer a menace for these *mohekuns* of the wilderness.

Following the sun of this first wonderful day came the moon and the stars of Baree's first real night. It was a splendid night, and with it a full red moon sailed up over the forests, flooding the earth with a new kind of light, softer and more beautiful to Baree. The wolf was strong in him, and he was restless. He had slept that day in the warmth of the sun, but he could not sleep in this glow of the moon. He nosed uneasily about Gray Wolf, who lay flat on her belly, her beautiful head alert, listening yearningly to the night sounds, and for the tonguing of Kazan, who had slunk away like a shadow to hunt.

Half a dozen times, as Baree wandered about near the windfall, he heard a soft whir over his head, and once or twice he saw gray shadows floating swiftly through the air. They were the big northern owls swooping down to investigate him, and if he had been a rabbit instead of a wolf-dog whelp, his first night under the moon and stars would have been his last; for unlike Wapoos, the rabbit, he was not cautious. Gray Wolf did not watch him closely. Instinct told her that in these forests there was no great danger for Baree except at the hands of man. In his veins ran the blood of the wolf. He was a hunter of all other wild creatures, but no other creature, either winged or fanged, hunted him.

In a way Baree sensed this. He was not afraid of the owls. He was not afraid of the strange blood-curdling cries they made in the black spruce-tops. But once fear entered into him, and he scurried back to his mother. It was when one of the winged hunters of the air swooped down on a snowshoe rabbit, and the squealing agony of the doomed creature set his heart thumping like a little hammer. He felt in those cries the nearness of that one ever-present tragedy of the wild—death. He felt it again that night when, snuggled close to Gray Wolf, he listened to the fierce outcry of a wolf pack that was close on the heels of a young caribou bull. And the meaning of it all, and the wild thrill of it all, came home to him early in the gray dawn when Kazan returned, holding between his jaws a huge rabbit that was still kicking and squirming with life.

This rabbit was the climax in the first chapter of Baree's education. It was as if Gray Wolf and Kazan had planned it all out, so that he might receive his first instruction in the art of killing. When Kazan had dropped it, Baree approached the big hare cautiously. The back of Wapoos, the rabbit, was broken. His round eyes were glazed, and he had ceased to feel pain. But to Baree, as he dug his tiny teeth into the heavy fur under Wapoo's throat, the hare was very much alive. The teeth did not go through into the flesh. With puppyish fierceness Baree hung on. He thought that he was killing. He could feel the dying convulsions of Wapoos. He could hear the last gasping breaths leaving the warm body, and he snarled and tugged until finally he fell back with a mouthful of fur. When he returned to the attack, Wapoos was quite dead, and Baree continued to bite and snarl until Gray Wolf came with her sharp fangs and tore the rabbit to pieces. After that followed the feast.

So Baree came to understand that to eat meant to kill, and as other days and nights passed, there grew in him swiftly the hunger for flesh. In this he was the true wolf. From Kazan he had taken other and stronger inheritances of the dog. He was magnificently black, which in later days gave him the name of *Kusketa Mohekun*—the black wolf. On his breast was a white star. His right ear was tipped with white. His tail, at six weeks, was bushy and hung low. It was a wolf's tail. His ears were Gray Wolf's ears—sharp, short, pointed, always alert. His foreshoulders gave promise of being splendidly like Kazan's, and when he stood up he was like the trace-dog, except that he always stood *sidewise* to the point or object he was watching. This, again, was the wolf, for a dog faces the direction in which he is looking intently.

One brilliant night, when Baree was two months old, and when the sky was filled with stars and a June moon so bright that it seemed scarcely higher than the tall spruce-tops, Baree settled back on his haunches and howled. It was a first effort. But there was no mistake in the note of it. It was the wolf howl. But a moment later when Baree slunk up to Kazan, as if deeply ashamed of his effort, he was wagging his tail in an unmistakably apologetic manner. And this again was the dog. If Tusoo, the dead Indian trapper, could have seen him then, he would have judged him by that wagging of his tail. It revealed the fact that deep in his heart—and in his soul, if we can concede that he had one—Baree was a dog.

In another way Tusoo would have found judgment of him. At two months the wolf whelp has forgotten how to play. He is a slinking part of the wilderness, already at work preying on creatures smaller and more helpless than himself. Baree still played. In his excursions away from the windfall he had never gone farther than the creek, a hundred yards from where his mother lay. He had helped to tear many dead and dying rabbits into pieces; he believed, if he thought upon the matter at all, that he was exceedingly fierce and courageous. But it was his ninth week before he

16

felt his spurs and fought his terrible battle with the young owl in the edge of the thick forest.

The fact that Oohoomisew, the big snow owl, had made her nest in a broken stub not far from the windfall was destined to change the whole course of Baree's life, just as the blinding of Gray Wolf had changed hers, and a man's club had changed Kazan's. The creek ran close past the stub, which had been riven by lightning; and this stub stood in a still, dark place in the forest, surrounded by tall, black spruce and enveloped in gloom even in broad day. Many times Baree had gone to the edge of this mysterious bit of forest and had peered in curiously, and with a growing desire.

On this day of his great battle its lure was overpowering. Little by little he entered into it, his eyes shining brightly and his ears alert for the slightest sounds that might come out of it. His heart beat faster. The gloom enveloped him more. He forgot the windfall and Kazan and Gray Wolf. Here before him lay the thrill of adventure. He heard stranger sounds, but very soft sounds, as if made by padded feet and downy wings, and they filled him with a thrilling expectancy. Under his feet there were no grass or weeds or flowers, but a wonderful brown carpet of soft evergreen needles. They felt good to his feet and were so velvety that he could not hear his own movement.

He was fully three hundred yards from the windfall when he passed Oohoomisew's stub and into a thick growth of young balsams. And there—directly in his path—crouched the monster!

Papayuchisew (Young Owl) was not more than a third as large as Baree. But he was a terrifying-looking object. To Baree he seemed all head and eyes. He could see no body at all. Kazan had never brought in anything like this, and for a full half-minute he remained very quiet, eyeing it speculatively. Papayuchisew did not move a feather. But as Baree advanced, a cautious step at a time, the bird's eyes grew bigger and the feathers about his head ruffled up as if stirred by a bit of wind. He came of a fighting family, this little Papayuchisew—a savage, fearless, and killing family—and even Kazan would have taken note of those ruffling feathers.

With a space of two feet between them, the pup and the owlet eyed each other. In that moment, if Gray Wolf could have seen, she might have said to Baree: "Use your legs—and run!" And Oohoomisew, the old owl, might have said to Papayuchisew: "You little fool—use your wings and fly!"

They did neither—and the fight began.

Papayuchisew started it, and with a single wild yelp Baree went back in a heap, the owlet's beak fastened like a red-hot vise in the soft flesh at the end of his nose. That one yelp of surprise and pain was Baree's first and last cry in the fight. The wolf surged in him; rage and the desire to kill possessed him. As Papayuchisew hung on, he made a curious hissing sound; and as Baree rolled and gnashed his teeth and fought to free himself from that amazing grip on his nose, fierce little snarls rose out of his throat.

For fully a minute Baree had no use of his jaws.

Then, by accident, he wedged Papayuchisew in a crotch of a low ground-shrub, and a bit of his nose gave way. He might have run then, but instead of that he was back at the owlet like a flash. Flop went Papayuchisew on his back, and Baree buried his needle-like teeth in the bird's breast. It was like trying to bite through a pillow, the feathers were so close and thick. Deeper and deeper Baree sank his fangs, and just as they were beginning to prick the owlet's skin, Papayuchisew—jabbing a little blindly with a beak that snapped sharply every time it closed—got him by the ear.

The pain of that hold was excruciating to Baree, and he made a more desperate effort to get his teeth through his enemy's thick armor of feathers. In the struggle they rolled under the low balsams to the edge of the ravine through which ran the creek. Over the steep edge they plunged, and as they rolled and bumped to the bottom, Baree loosed his hold. Papayuchisew hung valiantly on, and when they reached the bottom he still had his grip on Baree's ear.

Baree's nose was bleeding; his ear felt as if it were being pulled from his head; and in this uncomfortable moment a newly awakened instinct made Baby Papayuchisew discover his wings as a fighting asset. An owl has never really begun to fight until he uses his wings, and with a joyous hissing, Papayuchisew began beating his antagonist so fast and so viciously that Baree was dazed. He was compelled to close his eyes, and he snapped blindly. For the first time since the battle began he felt a strong inclination to get away.

He tried to tear himself free with his forepaws, but Papayuchisew—slow to reason but of firm conviction—hung to Baree's ear like grim fate.

At this critical point, when the understanding of defeat was forming itself swiftly in Baree's mind, chance saved him. His fangs closed on one of the owlet's tender feet. Papayuchisew gave a sudden squeak. The ear was free at last—and with a snarl of triumph Baree gave a vicious tug at Papayuchisew's leg.

In the excitement of battle he had not heard the rushing tumult of the creek close under them, and over the edge of a rock Papayuchisew and he went together, the chill water of the rain-swollen stream muffling a final snarl and a final hiss of the two little fighters.

CHAPTER III

TO Papayuchisew, after his first mouthful of water, the stream was almost as safe as the air, for he went sailing down it with the lightness of a gull, wondering in his slow-thinking big head why he was moving so swiftly and so pleasantly without any effort of his own.

To Baree it was a different matter. He went down almost like a stone. A mighty roaring filled his ears; it was dark, suffocating, terrible. In the swift current he was twisted over and over. For twenty feet he was under water. Then he rose to the surface and desperately began using his legs. It was of little use. He had only time to blink once or twice and catch a lungful of air when he shot into a current that was running like a millrace between the butts of two fallen trees, and for another twenty feet the sharpest eyes could not have seen hair or hide of him. He came up again at the edge of a shallow riffle over which the water ran like the rapids at Niagara in miniature, and for fifty or sixty yeards he was flung along like a hairy ball. From this he was hurled into a deep, cold pool; and then—half dead—he found himself crawling out on a gravelly bar.

For a long time Baree lay there in a pool of sunlight without moving. His ear hurt him; his nose was raw, and burned as if he had thrust it into fire. His legs and body were sore, and as he began to wander along the gravel bar, he was the most wretched pup in the world. He was also completely turned around. In vain he looked about him for some familiar mark—something that might guide him back to his windfall home. Everything was strange. He did not know that the water had flung him out on the wrong side of the stream, and that to reach the windfall he would have to cross it again. He whined, but that was as loud as his voice rose. Gray Wolf could have heard his barking, for the windfall was not more than two hundred and fifty yards up the stream. But the wolf in Baree held him silent, except for his low whining.

Striking the main shore, Baree began going downstream. This was away from the windfall, and each step that he took carried him farther and farther from home. Every little while he stopped and listened. The forest was deeper. It was growing blacker and more mysterious. Its silence was frightening. At the end of half an hour Baree would even have welcomed Papayuchisew. And he would not have fought him—he would have inquired, if possible, the way back home.

Baree was fully three-quarters of a mile from the windfall when he came to a point where the creek split itself into two channels. He had but one choice to follow—the stream that flowed a little south and east. This stream did not run swiftly. It was not filled with shimmering riffles, and rocks about which the water sang and foamed. It grew black, like the forest. It was still and deep. Without knowing it, Baree was burying himself deeper and deeper into Tusoo's old trapping grounds. Since Tusoo had died, they had lain undisturbed except for the wolves, for Gray Wolf and Kazan had not hunted on this side of the waterway—and the wolves themselves preferred the more open country for the chase.

Suddenly Baree found himself at the edge of a deep, dark pool in which the water lay still as oil, and his heart nearly jumped out of his body when a great, sleek, shining creature sprang out from almost under his nose and landed with a tremendous splash in the center of it. It was Nekik, the otter.

The otter had not heard Baree, and in another moment Napanekik, his wife, came sailing out of a patch of gloom, and behind her came three little otters, leaving behind them four shimmering wakes in the oily-looking water. What happened after that made Baree forget for a few minutes that he was lost. Nekik had disappeared under the surface, and now he came up directly under his unsuspecting mate with a force that lifted her half out of the water. Instantly he was gone again, and Napanekik took after him fiercely. To Baree it did not look like play. Two of the baby otters had pitched on the third, which seemed to be fighting desperately. The chill and ache went out of Baree's body. His blood ran excitedly; he forgot himself, and let out a bark. In a flash the otters disappeared. For several minutes the water in the pool continued to rock and heave—and that was all. After a little, Baree drew himself back into the bushes and went on.

It was about three o'clock in the afternoon, and the sun should still have been well up in the sky. But it was growing darker steadily, and the strangeness and fear of it all lent greater speed to Baree's legs. He stopped every little while to listen, and at one of these intervals he heard a sound that drew from him a responsive and joyous whine. It was a distant howl—a wolf's howl—straight ahead of him. Baree was not thinking of wolves but of Kazan, and he ran through the gloom of the forest until he was winded. Then he stopped and listened a long time. The wolf howl did not come again. Instead of it there rolled up from the west a deep and thunderous rumble. Through the tree-tops there flashed a vivid streak of lightning. A moaning whisper of wind rode in advance of the storm; the thunder grew nearer; and a second flash of lightning seemed searching Baree out where he stood shivering under a canopy of great spruce. This was his second storm. The first had frightened him terribly, and he had crawled far back into the shelter of the windfall. The best he could find now was a hollow under a big root, and into this he slunk, crying softly. It was a babyish cry, a cry for his mother, for home, for warmth, for something soft and protecting to nestle up to; and as he cried, the storm burst over the forest.

Baree had never before heard so much noise, and he had never seen the lightning play in such sheets of fire as when this June deluge fell. It seemed at times as though the whole world were aflame, and the earth seemed to shake and roll under the crashes of the thunder. He ceased his crying and made himself as small as he could under the root, which protected him partly from the terrific beat of the rain which came down through the treetops in a flood. It was now so black that except when the lightning ripped great holes in the gloom he could not see the spruce-trunks twenty feet away. Twice that distance from Baree there was a huge dead stub that stood out like a ghost each time the fires swept the sky, as if defying the flaming hands up there to strike—and strike, at last, one of them did! A bluish tongue of snapping flame ran down the old stub; and as it touched the earth, there came a tremendous explosion above the treetops. The massive stub shivered, and then it broke asunder as if cloven by a gigantic axe. It crashed down so close to

Baree that earth and sticks flew about him, and he let out a wild yelp of terror as he tried to crowd himself deeper into the shallow hole under the root.

With the destruction of the old stub the thunder and lightning seemed to have vented their malevolence. The thunder passed on into the south and east like the rolling of ten thousand heavy cartwheels over the roofs of the forest, and the lightning went with it. The rain fell steadily. The hole in which he had taken shelter was soppy. He was drenched; his teeth chattered as he waited for the next thing to happen.

It was a long wait. When the rain stopped, and the sky cleared, it was night. Through the tops of the trees Baree could have seen the stars if he had poked out his head and looked upward. But he clung to his hole. Hour after hour passed. Exhausted, half drowned, footsore, and hungry, he did not move. At last he fell into a troubled sleep, a sleep in which every now and then he cried softly and forlornly for his mother. When he ventured out from under the root it was morning, and the sun was shining.

At first Baree could hardly stand. His legs were cramped; every bone in his body seemed out of joint; his ear was stiff where the blood had oozed out of it and hardened, and when he tried to wrinkle his wounded nose, he gave a sharp little yap of pain. If such a thing were possible, he looked even worse than he felt. His hair had dried in muddy patches; he was dirt-stained from end to end; and where yesterday he had been plump and shiny, he was now as thin and wretched as misfortune could possibly make him. And he was hungry. He had never before known what it meant to be really hungry.

When he went on, continuing in the direction he had been following yesterday, he slunk along in a disheartened sort of way. His head and ears were no longer alert, and his curiosity was gone. He was not only stomach-hungry: mother-hunger rose above his physical yearning for something to eat. He wanted his mother as he had never wanted her before in his life. He wanted to snuggle his shivering little body close up to her and feel the warm caressing of her tongue and listen to the mothering whine of her voice. And he wanted Kazan, and the old windfall, and that big blue spot that was in the sky right over it. While he followed again along the edge of the creek, he whimpered for them as a child might grieve.

The forest grew more open after a time, and this cheered him up a little. Also the warmth of the sun was taking the ache out of his body. He grew hungrier and hungrier. He had depended entirely on Kazan and Gray Wolf for food. His parents had, in some ways, made a great baby of him. Gray Wolf's blindness accounted for this, for since his birth she had not taken up her hunting with Kazan, and it was quite natural that Baree should stick close to her, though more than once he had been filled with a great yearning to follow his father. Nature was hard at work trying to overcome its handicap now. It was struggling to impress on Baree that the time had now come when he must seek his own food. The fact impinged itself upon him slowly but steadily, and he began to think of the three or four shellfish he had caught and devoured on the stony creek bar near the windfall. He also remembered the open clamshell he had found, and the lusciousness of the tender morsel inside it. A new excitement began to possess him. He became, all at once, a hunter.

With the thinning out of the forest the creek grew more shallow. It ran again over bars of sand and stones, and Baree began to nose along the edge of these. For a long time he had no success. The few crayfish that he saw were exceedingly lively and elusive, and all the clamshells were shut so tight that even Kazan's powerful jaws would have had difficulty in smashing them. It was almost noon when he caught his first crayfish, about as big as a man's forefinger. He devoured it ravenously. The taste of food gave him fresh courage. He caught two more crayfish during the afternoon. It was almost dusk when he stirred a young rabbit out from under a cover of grass. If he had been a month older, he could have caught it. He was still very hungry, for three crayfish—scattered through the day— had not done much to fill the emptiness that was growing steadily in him.

With the approach of night Baree's fears and great loneliness returned. Before the day had quite gone he found himself a shelter under a big rock, where there was a warm, soft bed of sand. Since his fight with Papayuchisew, he had traveled a long distance, and the rock under which he made his bed this night was at least eight or nine miles from the windfall. It was in the open of the creek bottom, with the dark forest of spruce and cedars close on either side; and when the moon rose, and the stars filled the sky, Baree could look out and see the water of the stream shimmering in a glow almost as bright as day. Directly in front of him, running to the water's edge, was a broad carpet of white sand. Across this sand, half an hour later, came a huge black bear.

Until Baree had seen the otters at play in the creek, his conceptions of the forests had not gone beyond his own kind, and such creatures as owls and rabbits and small feathered things. The otters had not frightened him, because he still measured things by size, and Nekik was not half as big as Kazan. But the bear was a monster beside which Kazan would have stood a mere pygmy. He *was* big. If nature was taking this way of introducing Baree to the fact that there were more important creatures in the forests than dogs and wolves and owls and crayfish, she was driving the point home with a little more than necessary emphasis. For Wakayoo, the bear, weighed six hundred pounds if he weighed an ounce. He was fat and sleek from a month's feasting on fish. His shiny coat was like black velvet in the moonlight, and he walked with a curious rolling motion with his head hung low. The horror grew when he stopped broadside in the carpet of sand not more than ten feet from the rock under which Baree was shivering as if he had the ague.

It was quite evident that Wakayoo had caught scent of him in the air. Baree could hear him sniff—could hear his breathing—caught the starlight flashing in his reddish-brown eyes as they swung suspiciously

28

toward the big boulder. If Baree could have known then that *he*—his insignificant little self—was making that monster actually nervous and uneasy, he would have given a yelp of joy. For Wakayoo, in spite of his size, was somewhat of a coward when it came to wolves. And Baree carried the wolf scent. It grew stronger in Wakayoo's nose; and just then, as if to increase whatever nervousness was growing in him, there came from out of the forest behind him a long and wailing howl.

With an audible grunt, Wakayoo moved on. Wolves were pests, he argued. They wouldn't stand up and fight. They'd snap and yap at one's heels for hours at a time, and were always out of the way quicker than a wink when one turned on them. What was the use of hanging around where there were wolves, on a beautiful night like this? He lumbered on decisively. Baree could hear him splashing heavily through the water of the creek. Not until then did the wolf-dog draw a full breath. It was almost a gasp.

But the excitement was not over for the night. Baree had chosen his bed at a place where the animals came down to drink, and where they crossed from one of the creek forests to the other. Not long after the bear had disappeared he heard a heavy crunching in the sand, and hoofs rattling against stones, and a bull moose with a huge sweep of antlers passed through the open space in the moonlight. Baree stared with popping eyes, for if Wakayoo had weighed six hundred pounds, this gigantic creature whose legs were so long that it seemed to be walking on stilts weighed at least twice as much. A cow moose followed, and then a calf. The calf seemed all legs. It was too much for Baree, and he shoved himself farther and farther back under the rock until he lay wedged in like a sardine in a box. And there he lay until morning.

CHAPTER IV

WHEN Baree ventured forth from under his rock at the beginning of the next day, he was a much older puppy than when he met Papayuchisew, the young owl, in his path near the old windfall. If experience can be made to take the place of age, he had aged a great deal in the last forty-eight hours. In fact, he had passed almost out of puppyhood. He awoke with a new and much broader conception of the world. It was a big place. It was filled with many things, of which Kazan and Gray Wolf were not the most important. The monsters he had seen on the moonlit plot of sand had roused in him a new kind of caution, and the one greatest instinct of beasts—the primal understanding that it is the strong that prey upon the weak—was wakening swiftly in him. As yet he quite naturally measured brute force and the menace of things by size alone. Thus the bear was more terrible than Kazan, and the moose was more terrible than the bear.

It was quite fortunate for Baree that this instinct did not go to the limit in the beginning and make him understand that his own breed—the wolf—was most feared of all the creatures, claw, hoof, and wing, of the forests. Otherwise, like the small boy who thinks he can swim before he has mastered a stroke, he might somewhere have jumped in beyond his depth and had his head chewed off.

Very much alert, with the hair standing up along his spine, and a little growl in his throat, Baree smelled of the big footprints made by the bear and the moose. It was the bear scent that made him growl. He followed the tracks to the edge of the creek. After that he resumed his wandering, and also his hunt for food.

For two hours he did not find a crayfish. Then he came out of the green timber into the edge of a burned-over country. Here everything was black. The stumps of the trees stood up like huge charred canes. It was a comparatively fresh "burn" of last autumn, and the ash was still soft under Baree's feet. Straight through this black region ran the creek, and over it hung a blue sky in which the sun was shining. It was quite inviting to Baree. The fox, the wolf, the moose, and the caribou would have turned back from the edge of this dead country. In another year it would be good hunting ground, but now it was lifeless. Even the owls would have found nothing to eat out there.

It was the blue sky and the sun and the softness of the earth under his feet that lured Baree. It was pleasant to travel in after his painful experiences in the forest. He continued to follow the stream, though there was now little possibility of his finding anything to eat. The water had become sluggish and dark; the channel was choked with charred debris that had fallen into it when the forest had burned, and its shores were soft and muddy. After a time, when Baree stopped and looked about him, he could no longer see the green timber he had left. He was alone in that desolate wilderness of charred tree corpses. It was as still as death, too. Not the chirp of a bird broke the silence. In the soft ash he could not hear the fall of his own feet. But he was not frightened. There was the assurance of safety here.

If he could only find something to eat! That was the master thought that possessed Baree. Instinct had not yet impressed upon him that this which he saw all about him was starvation. He went on, seeking hopefully for food. But at last, as the hours passed, hope began to die out of him. The sun sank westward. The sky grew less blue; a low wind began to ride over the tops of the stubs, and now and then one of them fell with a startling crash.

Baree could go no farther. An hour before dusk he lay down in the open, weak and starved. The sun disappeared behind the forest. The moon rolled up from the east. The sky glittered with stars—and all through the night Baree lay as if dead. When morning came, he dragged himself to the stream for a drink. With his last strength he went on. It was the wolf urging him— compelling him to struggle to the last for his life. The dog in him wanted to lie down and die. But the wolf-spark in him burned stronger. In the end it won. Half a mile farther on he came again to the green timber.

In the forests as well as in the great cities fate plays its changing and whimsical hand. If Baree had dragged himself into the timber half an hour later he would have died. He was too far gone now to hunt for crayfish or kill the weakest bird. But he came just as Sekoosew, the ermine—the most bloodthirsty little pirate of all the wild—was making a kill.

That was fully a hundred yards from where Baree lay stretched out under a spruce, almost ready to give up the ghost. Sekoosew was a mighty hunter of his kind. His body was about seven inches long, with a tiny black-tipped tail appended to it, and he weighed perhaps five ounces. A baby's fingers could have encircled him anywhere between his four legs, and his little sharp-pointed head with its beady red eyes could slip easily through a hole an inch in diameter. For several centuries Sekoosew had helped to make history. It was he—when his pelt was worth a hundred dollars in king's gold—that lured the first shipload of gentlemen adventurers over the sea, with Prince Rupert at their head; it was little Sekoosew who was responsible for the forming of the great Hudson's Bay Company and the discovery of half a continent; for almost three centuries he had fought his fight for existence with the trapper. And now, though he was no longer worth his weight in yellow gold, he was the cleverest, the fiercest, and the most merciless of all the creatures that made up his world.

As Baree lay under his tree, Sekoosew was creeping on his prey. His game was a big fat spruce hen standing under a thicket of black currant bushes. The ear of no living thing could have heard Sekoosew's movement. He was like a shadow—a gray dot here, a flash there, now hidden behind a stick no larger than a man's wrist, appearing for a moment, the next instant gone as completely as if he had not existed. Thus he approached from fifty feet to within three feet of the spruce hen. That was his favorite striking distance. Unerringly he launched himself at the drowsy partridge's throat, and his needle-like teeth sank through feathers into flesh.

Sekoosew was prepared for what happened then. It always happened when he attacked Napanao, the wood partridge. Her wings were powerful, and her first instinct when he struck was always that of flight. She rose straight up now with a great thunder of wings. Sekoosew hung tight, his teeth buried deep in her throat, and his tiny, sharp claws clinging to her like hands. Through the air he whizzed with her, biting deeper and deeper, until a hundred yards from where that terrible death-thing had fastened to her throat, Napanao crashed again to earth.

Where she fell was not ten feet from Baree. For a few moments he looked at the struggling mass of feathers in a daze, not quite comprehending that at last food was almost within his reach. Napanao was dying, but she still struggled convulsively with her wings. Baree rose stealthily, and after a moment in which he gathered all his remaining strength, he made a rush for her. His teeth sank into her breast—and not until then did he see Sekoosew. The ermine had raised his head from the death grip at the partridge's throat, and his savage little red eyes glared for a single instant into Baree's. Here was something too big to kill, and with an angry squeak the ermine was gone. Napanao's wings relaxed, and the throb went out of her body. She was dead. Baree hung on until he was sure. Then he began his feast.

With murder in his heart, Sekoosew hovered near, whisking here and there but never coming nearer than half a dozen feet from Baree. His eyes were redder than ever. Now and then he emitted a sharp little squeak of rage. Never had he been so angry in all his life! To have a fat partridge stolen from him like this was an imposition he had never suffered before. He wanted to dart in and fasten his teeth in Baree's jugular. But he was too good a general to make the attempt, too good a Napoleon to jump deliberately to his Waterloo. An owl he would have fought. He might even have given battle to his big brother—and his deadliest enemy—the mink. But in Baree he recognized the wolf breed, and he vented his spite at a distance. After a time his good sense returned, and he went off on another hunt.

Baree ate a third of the partridge, and the remaining two-thirds he cached very carefully at the foot of the big spruce. Then he hurried down to the creek for a drink. The world looked very different to him now. After all, one's capacity for happiness depends largely on how deeply one has suffered. One's hard luck and misfortune form the measuring stick for future good luck and fortune. So it was with Baree. Forty-eight hours ago a full stomach would not have made him a tenth part as happy as he was now. Then his greatest longing was for his mother. Since then a still greater yearning had come into his life—for food. In a way it was fortunate for him that he had almost died of exhaustion and starvation, for his experience had helped to make a man of him—or a wolf-dog, just as you are of a mind to put it. He would miss his mother for a long time. But he would never miss her again as he had missed her yesterday, and the day before.

That afternoon Baree took a long nap close to his cache. Then he uncovered the partridge and ate his supper. When his fourth night alone came, he did not hide himself as he had done on the three preceding nights. He was strangely and curiously alert. Under the moon and the stars he prowled in the edge of the forest and out on the burn. He listened with a new kind of thrill to the faraway cry of a wolf pack on the hunt. He listened to the ghostly *whoo-whoo-whoo* of the owls without shivering. Sounds and silences were beginning to hold a new significant note for him.

For another day and night Baree remained in the vicinity of his cache. When the last bone was picked, he moved on. He now entered a country where subsistence was no longer a perilous problem for him. It was a lynx country, and where there are lynx, there are also a great many rabbits. When the rabbits thin out, the lynx emigrate to better hunting grounds. As the snowshoe rabbit breeds all the summer through, Baree found himself in a land of plenty. It was not difficult for him to catch and kill the young rabbits. For a week he prospered and grew bigger and stronger each day. But all the time, stirred by that seeking, wanderlust spirit—still hoping to find the old home and his mother—he traveled into the north and east.

And this was straight into the trapping country of Pierrot, the halfbreed.

Pierrot, until two years ago, had believed himself to be one of the most fortunate men in the big wilderness. That was before *La Mort Rouge*—The Red Death— came. He was half French, and he had married a Cree chief's daughter, and in their log cabin on the Gray Loon they had lived for many years in great prosperity and happiness. Pierrot was proud of three things in this wild world of his: he was immensely proud of Wyola, his royal-blooded wife; he was proud of his daughter; and he was proud of his reputation as a hunter. Until the Red Death came, life was quite complete for him. It was then—two years ago—that the smallpox killed his princess-wife. He still lived in the little cabin on the Gray Loon, but he was a different Pierrot. The heart was sick in him. It would have died, had it not been for Nepeese, his daughter. His wife had named her Nepeese, which means the Willow. Nepeese had grown up like the willow, slender as a reed, with all her mother's wild beauty, and with a little of the French thrown in. She was sixteen, with great, dark, wonderful eyes, and hair so beautiful that an agent from Montreal passing that way had once tried to buy it. It fell in two shining braids, each as big as a man's wrist, almost to her knees. *"Non, M'sieu,"* Pierrot had said, a cold glitter in his eyes as he saw what was in the agent's face. "It is not for barter."

Two days after Baree had entered his trapping ground, Pierrot came in from the forests with a troubled look in his face.

"Something is killing off the young beavers," he explained to Nepeese, speaking to her in French. "It is a lynx or a wolf. Tomorrow—" He shrugged his thin shoulders, and smiled at her.

"We will go on the hunt," laughed Nepeese happily, in her soft Cree.

When Pierrot smiled at her like that, and began with "Tomorrow," it always meant that she might go with him on the adventure he was contemplating.

Still another day later, at the end of the afternoon, Baree crossed the Gray Loon on a bridge of driftwood that had wedged between two trees. This was to the north. Just beyond the driftwood bridge there was a small open, and on the edge of this Baree paused to enjoy the last of the setting sun. As he stood motionless and listening, his tail drooping low, his ears alert, his sharp-pointed nose sniffing the new country to the north, there was not a pair of eyes in the forest that would not have taken him for a young wolf.

From behind a clump of young balsams, a hundred yards away, Pierrot and Nepeese had watched him come over the driftwood bridge. Now was the time, and Pierrot leveled his rifle. It was not until then that

Nepeese touched his arm softly. Her breath came a little excitedly as she whispered:

"Nootawe, let me shoot. I can kill him!"

With a low chuckle Pierrot gave the gun to her. He counted the whelp as already dead. For Nepeese, at that distance, could send a bullet into an inch square nine times out of ten. And Nepeese, aiming carefully at Baree, pressed steadily with her brown forefinger upon the trigger.

CHAPTER V

AS the Willow pulled the trigger of her rifle, Baree sprang into the air. He felt the force of the bullet before he heard the report of the gun. It lifted him off his feet, and then sent him rolling over and over as if he had been struck a hideous blow with a club. For a flash he did not feel pain. Then it ran through him like a knife of fire, and with that pain the dog in him rose above the wolf, and he let out a wild outcry of puppyish yapping as he rolled and twisted on the ground.

Pierrot and Nepeese had stepped from behind the balsams, the Willow's beautiful eyes shining with pride at the accuracy of her shot. Instantly she caught her breath. Her brown fingers clutched at the barrel of her rifle. The chuckle of satisfaction died on Pierrot's lips as Baree's cries of pain filled the forest.

"*Uchi Moosis!*" gasped Nepeese, in her Cree.

Pierrot caught the rifle from her.

"*Diable!* A dog—a puppy!" he cried.

He started on a run for Baree. But in their amazement they had lost a few seconds and Baree's dazed senses were returning. He saw them clearly as they came across the open—a new kind of monster of the forests! With a final wail he darted back into the deep shadows of the trees. It was almost sunset, and he ran for the thick gloom of the heavy spruce near the creek. He had shivered at sight of the bear and the moose, but for the first time he now sensed the real meaning of danger. And it was close after him. He could hear the crashing of the two-legged beasts in pursuit; strange cries were almost at his heels—and then suddenly he plunged without warning into a hole.

It was a shock to have the earth go out from under his feet like that, but Baree did not yelp. The wolf was dominant in him again. It urged him to remain where he was, making no move, no sound—scarcely breathing. The voices were over him; the strange feet almost stumbled in the hole where he lay. Looking out of his dark hiding-place, he could see one of his enemies. It was Nepeese, the Willow. She was standing so that a last glow of the day fell upon her face. Baree did not take his eyes from her. Above his pain there rose in him a strange and thrilling fascination. The girl put her two hands to her mouth, and in a voice that was

soft and plaintive and amazingly comforting to his terrified little heart, cried:

"*Uchimoo—Uchimoo—Uchimoo!*"

And then he heard another voice; and this voice,
too, was far less terrible than many sounds he had
listened to in the forests.

"We cannot find him, Nepeese," the voice was saying. "He has crawled off to die. It is too bad. Come."

Where Baree had stood in the edge of the open Pierrot paused and pointed to a birch sapling that had been
cut clean off by the Willow's bullet. Nepeese understood. The sapling, no larger than her thumb, had
turned her shot a trifle and had saved Baree from
instant death.

She turned again, and called:

"*Uchimoo—Uchimoo—Uchimoo!*"

Her eyes were no longer filled with the thrill of
slaughter.

"He would not understand that," said Pierrot, leading the way across the open. "He is wild—born of the
wolves. Perhaps he was of Koomo's lead bitch, who
ran away to hunt with the packs last winter."

"And he will die—"

"*Ayetun*—yes, he will die."

But Baree had no idea of dying. He was too tough
a youngster to be shocked to death by a bullet passing
through the soft flesh of his foreleg. That was what
had happened. His leg was torn to the bone, but the
bone itself was untouched. He waited until the moon
had risen before he crawled out of his hole.

His leg had grown stiff then; it had stopped bleeding, but his whole body was racked by a terrible pain. A dozen Papayuchisews, all holding tight to his ears and nose, could not have hurt him more. Every time he moved, a sharp twinge shot through him; and yet he persisted in moving. Instinctively he felt that by traveling away from the hole he would get away from danger. This was the best thing that could have happened to him, for a little later a porcupine came wandering along, chattering to itself in its foolish, good-humored way, and fell with a fat thud into the hole. Had Baree remained, he would have been so full of quills that he must surely have died.

In another way the exercise of travel was good for Baree. It gave his wound no opportunity to "set," as Pierrot would have said, for in reality his hurt was more painful than serious. For the first hundred yards he hobbled along on three legs, and after that he found that he could use his fourth by humoring it a great deal. He followed the creek for a half-mile. Whenever a bit of brush touched his wound, he would snap at it viciously, and instead of whimpering when he felt one of the sharp twinges shooting through him, an angry little growl gathered in his throat, and his teeth clicked. Now that he was out of the hole, the effect of the Willow's shot was stirring every drop of wolf-blood in his body. In him there was a growing animosity—a feeling of rage not against any one thing in particular, but against all things. It was not the feeling with which he had fought Papayuchisew, the young owl. On this night the dog in him had disappeared. An accumulation of misfortunes had descended upon him, and out of these misfortunes—and his present hurt—the wolf had risen savage and vengeful.

This was the first night Baree had traveled. He was, for the time, unafraid of anything that might creep up on him out of the darkness. The blackest shadows had lost their thrill. It was the first big fight between the two natures that were born in him—the wolf and the dog—and the dog was vanquished. Now and then he stopped to lick his wound, and as he licked it he growled, as though for the hurt itself he held a personal antagonism. If Pierrot could have seen and heard, he would have understood very quickly, and he would have said: "Let him die. The club will never take that devil out of him."

In this humor Baree came, an hour later, out of the heavy timber of the creek bottom into the more open spaces of a small plain that ran along the foot of a ridge. It was in this plain that Oohoomisew hunted. Oohoomisew was a huge snow owl. He was the patriarch among all the owls of Pierrot's trapping domain. He was so old that he was almost blind, and therefore he never hunted as other owls hunted. He did not hide himself in the black cover of spruce- and balsam-tops, or float softly through the night, ready in an instant to swoop down upon his prey. His eyesight was so poor that from a spruce-top he could not have seen a rabbit at all, and he might have mistaken a fox for a mouse.

So old Oohoomisew, learning wisdom from experience, hunted from ambush. He would squat on the ground, and for hours at a time he would remain there

43

without making a sound and scarcely moving a feather, waiting with the patience of Job for something to eat to come his way. Now and then he had made mistakes. Twice he had mistaken a lynx for a rabbit, and in the second attack he had lost a foot, so that when he slumbered aloft during the day he hung to his perch with one claw. Crippled, nearly blind, and so old that he had long ago lost the tufts of feathers over his ears, he was still a giant in strength, and when he was angry, one could hear the snap of his beak twenty yards away.

For three nights he had been unlucky, and tonight he had been particuarly unfortunate. Two rabbits had come his way, and he had lunged at each of them from his cover. The first he had missed entirely; the second had left with him a mouthful of fur—and that was all. He was ravenously hungry, and he was gritting his bill in his bad temper when he heard Baree approaching.

Even if Baree could have seen under the dark bush ahead, and had discovered Oohoomisew ready to dart from his ambush, it is not likely that he would have gone very far aside. His own fighting blood was up. He, too, was ready for war.

Very indistinctly Oohoomisew saw him at last, coming across the little open which he was watching. He squatted down. His almost sightless eyes glowed like two bluish pools of fire. Ten feet away, Baree stopped for a moment and licked his wound. Oohoomisew waited cautiously. Again Baree advanced, passing within six feet of the bush. With a swift hop and a sudden thunder of his powerful wings the great owl was upon him.

This time Baree let out no cry of pain or of fright. The wolf is *kipichi-mao*, as the Indians say. No hunter ever heard a trapped wolf whine for mercy at the sting of a bullet or the beat of a club. He dies with his fangs bared. Tonight it was a wolf whelp that Oohoomisew was attacking, and not a dog pup. The owl's first rush keeled Baree over, and for a moment he was smothered under the huge, outspread wings, while Oohoomisew—pinioning him down—hopped for a clawhold with his one good foot, and struck fiercely with his beak.

One blow of that beak anywhere about the head would have settled for a rabbit, but at the first thrust Oohoomisew discovered that it was not a rabbit he was holding under his wings. A blood-curdling snarl answered the blow, and Oohoomisew remembered the lynx, his lost foot, and his narrow escape with his life. The old pirate might have beaten a retreat, but Baree was no longer the puppyish Baree of that hour in which he had fought young Papayuchisew. Experience and hardship had aged and strengthened him; his jaws had passed quickly from the bone-licking to the bone-cracking age—and before Oohoomisew could get away, if he was thinking of flight at all, Baree's fangs closed with a vicious snap on his one good leg.

In the stillness of night there rose a still greater thunder of wings, and for a few moments Baree closed his eyes to keep from being blinded by Oohoomisew's furious blows. But he hung on grimly, and as his teeth met through the flesh of the old night pirate's leg, his angry snarl carried defiance to Oohoomisew's ears. Rare good fortune had given him that grip on the leg, and Baree knew that triumph or defeat depended on his ability to hold it. The old owl had no other claw to sink into him, and it was impossible—caught as he was—for him to tear at Baree with his beak. So he continued to beat that thunder of blows with his four-foot wings.

The wings made a great tumult about Baree, but they did not hurt him. He buried his fangs deeper. His snarls rose more fiercely as he got the taste of Oohoomisew's blood, and through him there surged more hotly the desire to kill this monster of the night, as though in the death of this creature he had the opportunity of avenging himself for all the hurts and hardships that had befallen him since he lost his mother.

Oohoomisew had never felt a great fear until now. The lynx had snapped at him but once—and was gone, leaving him crippled. But the lynx had not snarled in that wolfish way, and it had not hung on. A thousand and one nights Oohoomisew had listened to the wolf howl. Instinct had told him what it meant. He had seen the packs pass swiftly through the night, and always when they passed he had kept in the deepest shadows. To him, as for all other wild things, the wolf howl stood for death. But until now, with Baree's fangs buried in his leg, he had never sensed fully the wolf-fear. It had taken it years to enter into his slow, stupid head—but now that it was there, it possessed him as no other thing had ever possessed him in all his life.

Suddenly Oohoomisew ceased his beating and launched himself upward. Like huge fans his powerful wings churned the air, and Baree felt himself lifted suddenly from the earth. Still he held on—and in a moment both bird and beast fell back with a thud.

Oohoomisew tried again. This time he was more successful, and he rose fully six feet into the air with Baree. They fell again. A third time the old outlaw fought to wing himself free of Baree's grip; and then, exhausted, he lay with his giant wings outspread, hissing and cracking his bill.

Under those wings Baree's mind worked with the swift instincts of the killer. Suddenly he changed hold, burying his fangs into the under part of Oohoomisew's body. They sank into three inches of feathers. Swift as Baree had been, Oohoomisew was equally swift to take advantage of his opportunity. In an instant he had swooped upward. There was a jerk, a rending of feathers from flesh—and Baree was alone on the field of battle.

Baree had not killed, but he had conquered. His first great day—or night—had come. The world was filled with a new promise for him, as vast as the night itself. And after a moment he sat back on his haunches, sniffing the air for his beaten enemy; and then, as if defying the feathered monster to come back and fight to the end, he pointed his sharp little muzzle up to the stars and sent forth his first babyish wolf howl into the night.

CHAPTER VI

BAREE'S fight with Oohoomisew was good medicine for him. It not only gave him great confidence in himself, but it also cleared the fever of ugliness from his blood. He no longer snapped and snarled at things as he went on through the night.

It was a wonderful night. The moon was straight overhead, and the sky was filled with stars, so that in the open spaces the light was almost like that of day, except that it was softer and more beautiful. It was very still. There was no wind in the treetops, and it seemed to Baree that the howl he had given must have echoed to the end of the world.

Now and then Baree heard a sound—and always he stopped, attentive and listening. Far away he heard the long, soft mooing of a cow moose; he heard a great splashing in the water of a small lake that he came to, and once there came to him the sharp cracking of horn against horn—two bucks settling a little difference of opinion a quarter of a mile away. But it was always the wolf howl that made him sit and listen longest, his heart beating with a strange impulse which he did not as yet understand. It was the call of his breed, growing in him slowly but insistently.

He was still a wanderer—*pupamootao*, the Indians call it. It is this "wander spirit" that inspires for a time nearly every creature of the wild as soon as it is able to care for itself—nature's scheme, perhaps, for doing away with too close family relations and possibly dangerous interbreeding. Baree, like the young wolf seeking new hunting grounds, or the young fox discovering a new world, had no reason or method in his wandering. He was simply "traveling"—going on. He wanted something which he could not find. The wolf note brought it to him.

The stars and the moon filled Baree with a yearning for this something. The distant sounds impinged upon him his great aloneness. And instinct told him that only by questing could he find. It was not so much Kazan and Gray Wolf that he missed now—not so much motherhood and home as it was companionship. Now that he had fought the wolfish rage out of him in his battle with Oohoomisew, the dog part of him had come into its own again—the lovable half of him, the part that wanted to snuggle up near something that was alive and friendly, small odds whether it wore feather or fur, was clawed or hoofed.

He was sore from the Willow's bullet, and he was sore from battle, and toward dawn he lay down under a shelter of alders at the edge of a second small lake and rested until midday. Then he began questing in the reeds and close to the pond lilies for food. He found a dead jackfish, partly eaten by a mink, and finished it.

His wound was much less painful this afternoon, and by nightfall he scarcely noticed it at all. Since his almost tragic end at the hands of Nepeese, he had been traveling in a general northeasterly direction, following instinctively the run of the waterways; but his progress had been slow, and when darkness came again he was not more than eight or ten miles from the hole into which he had fallen after the Willow had shot him.

Baree did not travel far this night. The fact that his wound had come with dusk, and his fight with Oohoomisew still later, filled him with caution. Experience had taught him that the dark shadows and the black pits in the forest were possible ambuscades of danger. He was no longer afraid, as he had once been, but he had had fighting enough for a time, and so he accepted circumspection as the better part of valor and held himself aloof from the perils of darkness. It was a strange instinct that made him seek his bed on the top of a huge rock up which he had some difficulty in climbing. Perhaps it was a harkening back to the days of long ago when Gray Wolf, in her first motherhood, sought refuge at the summit of the Sun Rock, which towered high above the forest world of which she and Kazan were a part, and where later she was blinded in her battle with the lynx.

Baree's rock, instead of rising for a hundred feet or more straight up, was possibly as high as a man's head. It was in the edge of the creek bottom, with the spruce forest close at his back. For many hours he did not sleep, but lay keenly alert, his ears tuned to catch every sound that came out of the dark world about him. There was more than curiosity in his alertness tonight. His education had broadened immensely in one way: he had learned that he was a very small part of all this wonderful earth that lay under the stars and the moon, and he was keenly alive with the desire to become better acquainted with it without any more fighting or hurt. Tonight he knew what it meant when he saw now and then gray shadows float silently out of the forest into the moonlight—the owls, monsters of the breed with which he had fought. He heard the crackling of hoofed feet and the smashing of heavy bodies in the underbrush. He heard again the mooing of the moose. Voices came to him that he had not heard before—the sharp *yap-yap-yap* of a fox, the unearthly, laughing cry of a great northern loon on a lake half a mile away, the scream of a lynx that came floating through miles of forest, the low, soft croaks of the nighthawks between himself and the stars. He heard strange whisperings in the treetops—whisperings of the winds; and once, in the heart of a dead stillness, a buck whistled shrilly close behind his rock—and at the wolf scent in the air shot away in a terror-stricken gray streak.

All these sounds held their new meaning for Baree. Swiftly he was coming into his knowledge of the wilderness. His eyes gleamed; his blood thrilled. For many minutes at a time he scarcely moved. But of all the sounds that came to him, the wolf cry thrilled him most. Again and again he listened to it. At times it was far away, so far that it was like a whisper, dying away almost before it reached him; and then again it would come to him full-throated, hot with the breath of the chase, calling him to the red thrill of the hunt, to the wild orgy of torn flesh and running blood—calling, calling, calling. That was it, calling him to his own kin, to the bone of his bone and the flesh of his flesh—

to the wild, fierce hunting packs of his mother's tribe! It was Gray Wolf's voice seeking for him in the night— Gray Wolf's blood inviting him to the Brotherhood of the Pack.

Baree trembled as he listened. In his throat he whined softly. He edged to the sheer face of the rock. He wanted to go; nature was urging him to go. But the call of the wild was struggling against odds; for in him was the dog, with its generations of subdued and sleeping instincts—and all that night the dog in him kept Baree to the top of his rock.

Next morning Baree found many crayfish along the creek, and he feasted on their succulent flesh until he felt that he would never be hungry again. Nothing had tasted quite so good since he had eaten the partridge of which he had robbed Sekoosew the ermine.

In the middle of the afternoon Baree came into a part of the forest that was very quiet and very peaceful. The creek had deepened. In places its banks swept out until they formed small ponds. Twice he made considerable detours to get around these ponds. He traveled very quietly, listening and watching. Not since the ill-fated day he had left the old windfall had he felt quite so much at home as now. It seemed to him at last he was treading country which he knew, and where he would find friends. Perhaps this was another miracle-mystery of instinct—of nature. For he was in old Beaver-tooth's domain. It was here that his father and mother had hunted in the days before he was born. It was not far from here that Kazan and Beaver-tooth had fought that mighty duel underwater, from which Kazan had escaped with his life without another breath to lose.

Baree would never know these things. He would never know that he was traveling over old trails. But something deep in him gripped at him strangely. He sniffed the air, as if in it he found the scent of familiar things. It was only a faint breath—an indefinable promise that brought him to the point of a mysterious anticipation.

The forest grew deeper. It was wonderful. There was no undergrowth, and traveling under the trees was like being in a vast, mystery-filled cavern through the roof of which the light of day broke softly, brightened here and there by golden splashes of the sun. For a mile Baree made his way quietly through this forest. He saw nothing but a few winged flittings of birds; there was almost no sound. Then he came to a still larger pond. Around this pond there was a thick growth of alders and willows; the larger trees had thinned out. He saw the glimmer of afternoon sunlight on the water—and then, all at once, he heard life.

There had been few changes in Beaver-tooth's colony since the days of his feud with Kazan and the otters. Old Beaver-tooth was still older. He was fatter. He slept a great deal, and perhaps he was less cautious. He was dozing on the great mud-and-brushwood dam of which he had been engineer-in-chief, when Baree came out softly on a high bank thirty or forty feet away. So noiseless had Baree been that none of the beavers had seen or heard him. He squatted himself flat on his belly, hidden behind a tuft of grass, and with eager interest watched every movement. Beaver-tooth was rousing himself. He stood on his short legs for a moment; then he tilted himself up on his broad, flat tail like a soldier at attention, and with a sudden whistle dived into the pond with a great splash.

In another moment it seemed to Baree that the pond was alive with beavers. Heads and bodies appeared and disappeared, rushing this way and that through the water in a manner that amazed and puzzled him. It was the colony's evening frolic. Tails hit the water like flat boards. Odd whistlings rose above the splashing—and then as suddenly as it had begun, the play came to an end. There were probably twenty beavers, not counting the young, and as if guided by a common signal—something which Baree had not heard—they became so quiet that hardly a sound could be heard in the pond. A few of them sank under the water and disappeared entirely, but most of them Baree could watch as they drew themselves out on shore.

The beavers lost no time in getting at their labor, and Baree watched and listened without so much as rustling a blade of the grass in which he was concealed. He was trying to understand. He was striving to place these curious and comfortable-looking creatures in his knowledge of things. They did not alarm him; he felt no uneasiness at their number or size. His stillness was not the quiet of discretion, but rather of a strange and growing desire to get better acquainted with this curious four-legged brotherhood of the pond. Already they had begun to make the big forest less lonely for him. And then, close under him—

not more than ten feet from where he lay—he saw something that almost gave voice to the puppyish longing for companionship that was in him.

Down there, on a clean strip of the shore that rose out of the soft mud of the pond, waddled fat little Umisk and three of his playmates. Umisk was just about Baree's age, perhaps a week or two younger. But he was fully as heavy, and almost as wide as he was long. Nature can produce no four-footed creature that is more lovable than a baby beaver, unless it is a baby bear; and Umisk would have taken first prize at any beaver baby show in the world. His three companions were a bit smaller. They came waddling from behind a low willow, making queer little chuckling noises, their little flat tails dragging like tiny sledges behind them. They were fat and furry, and mighty friendly-looking to Baree, and his heart beat a sudden swift *pit-a-pat* of joy.

But Baree did not move. He scarcely breathed. And then, suddenly, Umisk turned on one of his playmates and bowled him over. Instantly the other two were on Umisk, and the four little beavers rolled over and over, kicking with their short feet and spatting with their tails, and all the time emitting soft little squeaking cries. Baree knew that it was not fight but frolic. He rose up on his feet. He forgot where he was—forgot everything in the world but those playing, furry balls. For the moment all the hard training nature had been giving him was lost. He was no longer a fighter, no longer a hunter, no longer a seeker after food. He was a puppy, and in him there rose a desire that was greater than hunger. He wanted to go down there with Umisk and his little chums and roll and play. He wanted to tell them, if such a thing were possible, that he had lost his mother and his home, and that he had been having a mighty hard time of it, and that he would like to stay with them and their mothers and fathers if they didn't care.

In his throat there came the least bit of a whine. It was so low that Umisk and his playmates did not hear it. They were tremendously busy.

Softly Baree took his first step toward them, and then another—and at last he stood on the narrow strip of shore within half a dozen feet of them. His sharp little ears were pitched forward, and he was wiggling his tail as fast as he could, and every muscle in his body was trembling in anticipation.

It was then that Umisk saw him, and his fat little body became suddenly as motionless as a stone.

"Hello!" said Baree, wiggling his whole body and talking as plainly as a human tongue could talk. "Do you care if I play with you?"

Umisk made no response. His three playmates now had their eyes on Baree. They didn't make a move. They looked stunned. Four pairs of staring, wondering eyes were fixed on the stranger.

Baree made another effort. He groveled on his fore-legs, while his tail and hind legs continued to wiggle, and with a sniff he grabbed a bit of stick between his teeth.

"Come on—let me in," he urged. "I know how to play!"

56

He tossed the stick in the air as if to prove what he was saying, and gave a little yap.

Umisk and his brothers were like dummies.

And then, of a sudden, someone saw Baree. It was a big beaver swimming down the pond with a sapling timber for the new dam that was under way. Instantly he loosed his hold and faced the shore. And then, like the report of a rifle, there came the crack of his big flat tail on the water—the beaver's signal of danger that on a quiet night can be heard half a mile away.

"Danger," it warned. *"Danger—danger—danger!"*

Scarcely had the signal gone forth when tails were cracking in all directions—in the pond, in the hidden canals, in the thick willows and alders. To Umisk and his companions they said:

"Run for your lives!"

Baree stood rigid and motionless now. In amazement he watched the four little beavers plunge into the pond and disappear. He heard the sounds of other and heavier bodies striking the water. And then there followed a strange and disquieting silence. Softly Baree whined, and his whine was almost a sobbing cry. Why had Umisk and his little mates run away from him? What had he done that they didn't want to make friends with him? A great loneliness swept over him—a loneliness greater even than that of his first night away from his mother. The last of the sun faded out of the sky as he stood there. Darker shadows crept over the pond. He looked into the forest, where night was gathering—and with another whining cry he slunk back into it. He had not found friendship. He had not found comrade-ship. And his heart was very sad.

CHAPTER VII

FOR two or three days Baree's excursions after food took him farther and farther away from the pond. But each afternoon he returned to it—until the third day, when he discovered a new creek, and Wakayoo. The creek was fully two miles back in the forest. This was a different sort of stream. It sang merrily over a gravelly bed and between chasm walls of split rock. It formed deep pools and foaming eddies, and where Baree first struck it, the air trembled with the distant thunder of a waterfall. It was much pleasanter than the dark and silent beaver stream. It seemed possessed of life, and the rush and tumult of it—the song and thunder of the water—gave to Baree entirely new sensations. He made his way along it slowly and cautiously, and it was because of this slow-ness and caution that he came suddenly and unob-served upon Wakayoo, the big black bear, hard at work fishing.

Wakayoo stood knee-deep in a pool that had formed behind a sandbar, and he was having tremendously good luck. Even as Baree shrank back, his eyes pop-ping at sight of this monster he had seen but once before, in the gloom of night, one of Wakayoo's big paws sent a great splash of water high in the air, and a fish landed on the pebbly shore. A little while before, the suckers had run up the creek in thousands to spawn, and the rapid lowering of the water had caught many of them in these prison-pools. Wakayoo's fat, sleek body was evidence of the prosperity this circumstance had brought him. Although it was a little past the "prime" season for bearskins, Wakayoo's coat was splendidly thick and black.

For a quarter of an hour Baree watched him while he knocked fish out of the pool. When at last he stopped, there were twenty or thirty fish among the stones, some of them dead and others still flopping. From where he lay flattened out between two rocks, Baree could hear the crunching of flesh and bone as the bear devoured his dinner. It sounded good, and the fresh smell of fish filled him with a craving that had never been roused by crayfish or even partridge.

In spite of his fat and his size, Wakayoo was not a glutton, and after he had eaten his fourth fish he pawed all the others together in a pile, partly covered them by raking up sand and stones with his long claws, and finished his work of caching by breaking down a small balsam sapling so that the fish were entirely concealed. Then he lumbered slowly away in the direction of the rumbling waterfall.

Twenty seconds after the last of Wakayoo had disappeared in a turn of the creek, Baree was under the broken balsam. He dragged out a fish that was still alive. He ate the whole of it, and it was delicious.

59

Baree now found that Wakayoo had solved the food problem for him, and this day he did not return to the beaver pond, nor the next. The big bear was incessantly fishing up and down the creek, and day after day Baree continued his feasts. It was not difficult for him to find Wakayoo's caches. All he had to do was to follow along the shore of the stream, sniffing carefully. Some of the caches were getting old, and their perfume was anything but pleasant to Baree. These he avoided—but he never missed a meal or two out of a fresh one.

For a week life continued to be exceedingly pleasant. And then came the break—the change that was destined to mean as much for Baree as that other day, long ago, had meant for Kazan, his father, when he killed the man-brute in the edge of the wilderness.

This change came on the day when, in trotting around a great rock near the waterfall, Baree found himself face to face with Pierrot the hunter and Nepeese, the star-eyed girl who had shot him in the edge of the clearing.

It was Nepeese whom he saw first. If it had been Pierrot, he would have turned back quickly. But again the blood of his forebear was rousing strange tremblings within him. Was it like this that the first woman had looked to Kazan?

Baree stood still. Nepeese was not more than twenty feet from him. She sat on a rock, full in the early-morning sun, and was brushing out her wonderful hair. Her lips parted. Her eyes shone in an instant like stars. One hand remained poised, weighted with the jet tresses. She recognized him. She saw the white star on his breast and the white tip on his ear, and under her breath she whispered *"Uchi moosis!"*—"The dog pup!" It was the wild dog she had shot—and thought had died!

The evening before Pierrot and Nepeese had built a shelter of balsams behind the big rock, and on a small white plot of sand Pierrot was kneeling over a fire preparing breakfast while the Willow arranged her hair. He raised his head to speak to her, and saw Baree. In that instant the spell was broken. Baree saw the man-beast as he rose to his feet. Like a shot he was gone.

Scarcely swifter was he than Nepeese.

"Dépêchez-vous, mon père!" she cried. "It is the dog pup! Quick—"

In the floating cloud of her hair she sped after Baree like the wind. Pierrot followed, and in going he caught up his rifle. It was difficult for him to catch up with the Willow. She was like a wild spirit, her little moccasined feet scarcely touching the sand as she ran up the long bar. It was wonderful to see the lithe swiftness of her, and that wonderful hair streaming out in the sun. Even now, in this moment's excitement, it made Pierrot think of McTaggart, the Hudson's Bay Company's factor over at Lac Bain, and what he had said yesterday. Half the night Pierrot had lain awake, gritting his teeth at thought of it; and this morning, before Baree ran upon them, he had looked at Nepeese more closely than ever before in his life. She *was* beautiful. She was lovelier even than Wyola, her princess-mother, who was dead. That hair—which made men stare as if they could not believe! Those eyes—like pools filled with wonderful starlight! Her slimness, that was like a flower! And McTaggart had said—

Floating back to him there came an excited cry.

"Hurry, Nootawe! He has turned into the blind canyon. He cannot escape us now."

She was panting when he came up to her. The French blood in her glowed a vivid crimson in her cheeks and lips. Her white teeth gleamed like milk.

"In there!" And she pointed.

They went in.

Ahead of them Baree was running for his life. He sensed instinctively the fact that these wonderful two-legged beings he had looked upon were all-powerful. And they were after him! He could hear them. Nepeese was following almost as swiftly as he could run. Suddenly he turned into a cleft between two great rocks. Twenty feet in, his way was barred, and he ran back. When he darted out, straight up the canyon, Nepeese was not a dozen yards behind him, and he saw Pierrot almost at her side. The Willow gave a cry.

"Mana—mana—there he is!"

She caught her breath, and darted into a copse of young balsams where Baree had disappeared. Like a great entangling web her loose hair impeded her in the brush, and with an encouraging cry to Pierrot she stopped to gather it over her shoulder as he ran past her. She lost only a moment or two, and was after him. Fifty yards ahead of her Pierrot gave a warning shout. Baree had turned. Almost in the same breath he was tearing over his back trail, directly toward the Willow. He did not see her in time to stop or swerve aside, and Nepeese flung herself down in his path. For an instant or two they were together. Baree felt the smother of her hair, and the clutch of her hands. Then he squirmed away and darted again toward the blind end of the canyon.

Nepeese sprang to her feet. She was panting—and laughing. Pierrot came back wildly, and the Willow pointed beyond him.

"I had him—and he didn't bite!" she said, breathing swiftly. She still pointed to the end of the canyon, and she said again: "I had him—and he didn't bite me, Nootawe!"

That was the wonder of it. She had been reckless— and Baree had not bitten her! It was then, with her eyes shining at Pierrot, and the smile fading slowly from her lips, that she spoke softly the word *"Baree,"* which in her tongue meant "the wild dog"—a little brother of the wolf.

"Come," cried Pierrot, "or we will lose him!"

Pierrot was confident. The canyon had narrowed. Baree could not get past them unseen. Three minutes later Baree came to the blind end of the canyon—a wall of rock that rose straight up like the curve of a dish. Feasting on fish and long hours of sleep had fattened him, and he was half winded as he sought vainly for an exit. He was at the far end of the dishlike curve of rock, without a bush or a clump of grass to hide him, when Pierrot and Nepeese saw him again. Nepeese made straight toward him. Pierrot, foreseeing what Baree would do, hurried to the left, at right angles to the end of the canyon.

In and out among the rocks Baree sought swiftly for a way of escape. In a moment more he had come to the "box," or cup of the canyon. This was a break in the wall, fifty or sixty feet wide, which opened into a natural prison about an acre in extent. It was a beautiful spot. On all sides but that leading into the coulee it was shut in by walls of rock. At the far end a waterfall broke down in a series of rippling cascades. The grass was thick underfoot and strewn with flowers. In this trap Pierrot had got more than one fine haunch of venison. From it there was no escape, except in the face of his rifle. He called to Nepeese as he saw Baree entering it, and together they climbed the slope.

Baree had almost reached the edge of the little prison-meadow when suddenly he stopped himself so quickly that he fell back on his haunches, and his heart jumped up into his throat.

Full in his path stood Wakayoo, the huge black bear!

For perhaps a half-minute Baree hesitated between the two perils. He heard the voices of Nepeese and Pierrot. He caught the rattle of stones under their feet. And he was filled with a great dread. Then he looked at Wakayoo. The big bear had not moved an inch. He, too, was listening. But to him there was a thing more disturbing than the sounds he heard. It was the scent which he caught in the air—the man-scent.

Baree, watching him, saw his head swing slowly even as the footsteps of Nepeese and Pierrot became more and more distinct. It was the first time Baree had ever stood face to face with the big bear. He had watched him fish; he had fattened on Wakayoo's prowess; he had held him in splendid awe. Now there was something about the bear that took away his fear and gave him in its place a new and thrilling confidence. Wakayoo, big and powerful as he was, would not run from the two-legged creatures who pursued him! If Baree could only get past Wakayoo he was safe!

Baree darted to one side and ran for the open meadow. Wakayoo did not stir as Baree sped past him—no more than if he had been a bird or a rabbit. Then came another breath of air, heavy with the scent of man. This, at last, put life into him. He turned and began lumbering after Baree into the meadow-trap. Baree, looking back, saw him coming—and thought it was pursuit. Nepeese and Pierrot came over the slope, and at the same instant they saw both Wakayoo and Baree.

Where they entered into the grassy dip under the rock walls, Baree turned sharply to the right. Here was a great boulder, one end of it tilted up off the earth. It looked like a splendid hiding-place, and Baree crawled under it.

But Wakayoo kept straight ahead into the meadow.

From where he lay Baree could see what happened. Scarcely had he crawled under the rock when Nepeese and Pierrot appeared through the break in the dip, and stopped. The fact that they stopped thrilled Baree. They were afraid of Wakayoo! The big bear was two-thirds of the way across the meadow. The sun fell on him, so that his coat shone like black satin. Pierrot stared at him for a moment. Pierrot did not kill for the love of killing. Necessity made him a conservationist. But he saw that in spite of the lateness of the season, Wakayoo's coat was splendid—and he raised his rifle.

Baree saw this action. He saw, a moment later, something spit from the end of the gun, and then he heard that deafening crash that had come with his own hurt, when the Willow's bullet had burned through his flesh. He turned his eyes swiftly to Wakayoo. The big bear had stumbled; he was on his knees; and then he struggled up and lumbered on.

The roar of the rifle came again, and a second time Wakayoo went down. Pierrot could not miss at that distance. Wakayoo made a splendid mark. It was slaughter; yet for Pierrot and Nepeese it was business—the business of life.

Baree was shivering. It was more from excitement than fear, for he had lost his own fear in the tragedy of these moments. A low whine rose in his throat as he looked at Wakayoo, who had risen again and faced his enemies—his jaws gaping, his head swinging slowly, his legs weakening under him as the blood poured through his torn lungs. Baree whined—because Wakayoo had fished for him, because he had come to look on him as a friend, and because he knew it was death that Wakayoo was facing now. There was a third shot—the last. Wakayoo sank down in his tracks. His big head dropped between his forepaws. A racking cough or two came to Baree. And then there was silence.

It was slaughter—but business.

A minute later, standing over Wakayoo, Pierrot said to Nepeese:

"*Mon Dieu*, but it is a fine skin, *Sakahet*! It is worth twenty dollars over at Lac Bain!"

He drew forth his knife and began whetting it on a stone which he carried in his pocket. In these minutes Baree might have crawled out from under his rock and escaped down the canyon; for a space he was forgotten. Then Nepeese thought of him, and in that same strange, wondering voice she spoke again the word "*Baree.*"

Pierrot, who was kneeling, looked up at her.

"*Oui, Sakahet*. He was born of the wild. And now he is gone—"

The Willow shook her head.

"*Non*, he is not gone," she said, and her dark eyes quested the sunlit meadow.

CHAPTER VIII

AS Nepeese gazed about the rock-walled end of the canyon, the prison into which they had driven Wakayoo and Baree, Pierrot looked up again from his skinning of the big black bear, and he muttered something that no one but himself could have heard. "*Non*, it is not possible," he had said a moment before; but to Nepeese it was possible—the thought that was in her mind. It was a wonderful thought. It thrilled her to the depth of her wild, beautiful soul. It sent a glow into her eyes and a deeper flush of excitement into her cheeks and lips.

As she quested the ragged edges of the little meadow for signs of the dog pup, her thoughts flashed back swiftly. Two years ago they had buried her princess-mother under the tall spruce near their cabin. That day Pierrot's sun had set for all time, and her own life was filled with a vast loneliness. There had been three at the graveside that afternoon as the sun went down—Pierrot, herself, and a dog, a great, powerful husky with a white star on his breast and a white-tipped ear. He had been her dead mother's pet from puppyhood—her bodyguard, with her always, even with his head resting on the side of her bed as she died. And that night, the night of the day they buried her, the dog had disappeared. He had gone as quietly and as completely as her spirit. No one ever saw him after that. It was strange, and to Pierrot it was a miracle. Deep in his heart he was filled with the wonderful conviction that the dog had gone with his beloved Wyola into heaven.

But Nepeese had spent three winters at the Missioner's school at Nelson House. She had learned a great deal about white people and the real God, and she knew that Pierrot's thought was impossible. She believed that her mother's husky was either dead or had joined the wolves. Probably he had gone to the wolves. So—was it not possible that this youngster she and her father had pursued was of the flesh and blood of her mother's pet? It was more than possible. The white star on his breast, the white-tipped ear—the fact that he had not bitten her when he might easily have buried his fangs in the soft flesh of her arms! She was convinced. While Pierrot skinned the bear, she began hunting for Baree.

Baree had not moved an inch from under his rock. He lay there like a thing stunned, his eyes fixed steadily on the scene of the tragedy out in the meadow. He had seen something that he would never forget—even as he would never quite forget his mother and Kazan and the old windfall. He had witnessed the death of the creature he had thought all-powerful. Wakayoo, the big bear, had not even put up a fight. Pierrot and Nepeese had killed him *without touching him;* now Pierrot was cutting him with a knife which shot silvery flashes in the sun; and Wakayoo made no movement. It made Baree shiver, and he drew himself an inch farther back under the rock, where he was already wedged as if he had been shoved there by a strong hand.

He could see Nepeese. She came straight back to the break through which his flight had taken him, and stood at last not more than twenty feet from where he was hidden. Now that she stood where he could not escape, she began weaving her shining hair into two thick braids. Baree had taken his eyes from Pierrot, and he watched her curiously. He was not afraid now. His nerves tingled. In him a strange and growing force was struggling to solve a great mystery—the reason for his desire to creep out from under his rock and approach that wonderful creature with the shining eyes and the beautiful hair.

Baree wanted to approach. It was like an invisible string tugging at his very heart. It was Kazan, and not Gray Wolf, calling to him back through the centuries, a "call" that was as old as the Egyptian pyramids and perhaps ten thousand years older. But against that desire Gray Wolf was pulling from out the black ages of the forests. The wolf held him quiet and motionless. Nepeese was looking about her. She was smiling. For a moment her face was turned toward him, and he saw the white shine of her teeth, and her beautiful eyes seemed glowing straight at him.

And then, suddenly, she dropped on her knees and peered under the rock.

Their eyes met. For at least half a minute there was not a sound. Nepeese did not move, and her breath came so softly that Baree could not hear it.

Then she said, almost in a whisper:

"Baree! Baree! Upi Baree!"

It was the first time Baree had heard his name, and there was something so soft and assuring in the sound of it that in spite of himself the dog in him responded to it in a whimper that just reached the Willow's ear. Slowly she stretched in an arm. It was bare and round and soft. He might have darted forward the length of his body and buried his fangs in it easily. But something held him back. He knew that it was not an enemy; he knew that the dark eyes shining at him so wonderfully were not filled with the desire to harm—

70

and the voice that came to him softly was like a strange and thrilling music.

"Baree! Baree! Upi Baree!"

Over and over again the Willow called to him like that, while on her face she tried to draw herself a few inches farther under the rock. She could not reach him. There was still a foot between her hand and Baree, and she could not wedge herself in an inch more. And then she saw where on the other side of the rock there was a hollow, shut in by a stone. If she had removed the stone, and come in that way—

She drew herself out and stood once more in the sunshine. Her heart thrilled. Pierrot was busy over his bear—and she would not call him. She made an effort to move the stone which closed in the hollow under the big boulder, but it was wedged in tightly. Then she began digging with a stick. If Pierrot had been there, his sharp eyes would have discovered the significance of that stone, which was not larger than a water pail. Possibly for centuries it had lain there, its support keeping the huge rock from toppling down, just as an ounce-weight may swing the balance of a wheel that weighs a ton.

Five minutes—and Nepeese could move the stone. She tugged at it. Inch by inch she dragged it out until at last it lay at her feet and the opening was ready for her body. She looked again toward Pierrot. He was still busy, and she laughed softly as she untied a big red-and-white Bay handkerchief from about her shoulders. With this she would secure Baree. She dropped on her

71

hands and knees and then lowered herself flat on the ground and began crawling into the hollow under the boulder.

Baree had moved. With the back of his head flattened against the rock, he had heard something which Nepeese had not heard; he had felt a slow and growing pressure, and from this pressure he had dragged himself slowly—and the pressure still followed. The mass of rock was settling! Nepeese did not see or hear or understand. She was calling to him more and more pleadingly:

"*Baree—Baree—Baree—*"

Her head and shoulders and both arms were under the rock now. The glow of her eyes was very close to Baree. He whined. The thrill of a great and impending danger stirred in his blood. And then—

In that moment Nepeese felt the pressure of the rock on her shoulder, and into the eyes that had been glowing softly at Baree there shot a sudden wild look of horror. And then there came from her lips a cry that was not like any other sound Baree had ever heard in the wilderness—wild, piercing, filled with agonized fear. Pierrot did not hear that first cry. But he heard the second and the third—and then scream after scream as the Willow's tender body was slowly crushed under the settling mass. He ran toward it with the speed of the wind. The cries were weaker—dying away. He saw Baree as he came out from under the rock and ran into the canyon, and in the same instant he saw a part of the Willow's dress and her moccasined feet. The rest of her was hidden under the death trap.

Like a madman Pierrot began digging. When a few moments later he drew Nepeese out from under the boulder she was white and deathly still. Her eyes were closed. His hand could not feel that she was living, and a great moan of anguish rose out of his soul. But he knew how to fight for a life. He tore open her dress and found that she was not crushed as he had feared. Then he ran for water. When he returned, the Willow's eyes were open and she was gasping for breath.

"The blessed saints be praised!" sobbed Pierrot, falling on his knees at her side. *"Nepeese, ma Nepeese!"*

She smiled at him, with her two hands on her bare breast, and Pierrot hugged her up to him, forgetting the water he had run so hard to get.

Still later, when he got down on his knees and peered under the rock, his face turned white and he said: *"Mon Dieu,* if it had not been for that little hollow in the earth, Nepeese—"

He shuddered, and said no more. But Nepeese, happy in her salvation, made a movement with her hand and said, smiling at him: "I would have been like—*that.* Ah, *mon père,* I hope I shall never have a lover like that rock!"

Pierrot's face darkened as he bent over her.

"Non!" he said fiercely. "Never!"

He was thinking again of McTaggart, the factor at Lac Bain, and his hands clenched while his lips softly touched the Willow's hair.

73

CHAPTER IX

IMPELLED by the wild alarm of the Willow's terrible cries and the sight of Pierrot dashing madly toward him from the dead body of Wakayoo, Baree did not stop running until it seemed as though his lungs could not draw another breath. When he stopped, he was well out of the canyon and headed for the beaver pond. For almost a week Baree had not been near the pond. He had not forgotten Beaver-tooth and Umisk and the other little beavers, but Wakayoo and his daily catch of fresh fish had been too big a temptation for him. Now Wakayoo was gone. He sensed the fact that the big black bear would never fish again in the quiet pools and shimmering eddies, and that where for many days there had been peace and plenty, there was now great danger; and just as in another country he would have fled for safety to the old windfall, he now fled desperately for the beaver pond.

Exactly wherein lay Baree's fears it would be difficult to say—but surely it was not because of Nepeese. The Willow had chased him hard. She had flung herself upon him. He had felt the clutch of her hands and the smother of her soft hair, and yet of her he was not afraid! If he stopped now and then in his flight and looked back, it was to see if Nepeese was following. He would not have run hard from her—alone. Her eyes and voice and hands had set something stirring in him; he was filled with a greater yearning and a greater loneliness now—and that night he dreamed troubled dreams.

He found himself a bed under a spruce root not far from the beaver pond, and all through the night his sleep was filled with that restless dreaming—dreams of his mother, of Kazan, the old windfall, of Umisk— and of Nepeese. Once, when he awoke, he thought the spruce root was Gray Wolf; and when he found that she was not there, Pierrot and the Willow could have told what his crying meant if they had heard it. Again and again he had visions of the thrilling happenings of that day. He saw the flight of Wakayoo over the little meadow—he saw him die again. He saw the glow of the Willow's eyes close to his own, heard her voice—so sweet and low that it was like strange music to him—and again he heard her terrible screams.

Baree was glad when the dawn came. He did not seek for food, but went down to the pond. There was little hope and anticipation in his manner now. He remembered that, as plainly as animal ways could talk, Umisk and his playmates had told him they wanted nothing to do with him. And yet the fact that they were there took away some of his loneliness. It was more than loneliness. The wolf in him was submerged. The dog was master. And in these passing moments, when the blood of the wild was almost dormant in him, he was depressed by the instinctive and growing feeling that he was not of that wild, but a fugitive in it, menaced on all sides by strange dangers.

Deep in the northern forests the beaver does not work and play in darkness only, but uses day even more than night, and many of Beaver-tooth's people were awake when Baree began disconsolately to investigate the shores of the pond. The little beavers were still with their mothers in the big houses that looked like great domes of sticks and mud out in the middle of the lake. There were three of these houses, one of them at least twenty feet in diameter. Baree had some difficulty in following his side of the pond. When he got back among the willows and alders and birch, dozens of little canals crossed and crisscrossed in his path. Some of these canals were a foot wide, and others three or four feet, and all were filled with water. No country in the world ever had a better system of traffic than this domain of the beavers, down which they brought their working materials and food into the main reservoir—the pond.

In one of the larger canals Baree surprised a big beaver towing a four-foot cutting of birch as thick through as a man's leg—half a dozen breakfasts and dinners and suppers in that one cargo. The four or five inner barks of the birch are what might be called the bread and butter and potatoes of the beaver menu, while the more highly prized barks of the willow and young alder take the place of meat and pie.

Baree smelled curiously of the birch cutting after the old beaver had abandoned it in flight, and then went on. He did not try to hide himself now, and at least half a dozen beavers had a good look at him before he came to the point where the pond narrowed down to the width of the stream, almost half a mile from the dam. Then he wandered back. All that morning he hovered about the pond, showing himself openly.

In their big mud-and-stick strongholds the beavers held a council of war. They were distinctly puzzled. There were four enemies which they dreaded above all others: the otter, who destroyed their dams in the wintertime and brought death to them from cold and by lowering the water so they could not get to their food supplies; the lynx, who preyed on them all, young and old alike; and the fox and wolf, who would lie in ambush for hours in order to pounce on the very young, like Umisk and his playmates. If Baree had been any one of these four, wily Beaver-tooth and his people would have known what to do. But Baree was surely not an otter, and if he was a fox or a wolf or a lynx, his actions were very strange, to say the least. Half a dozen times he had had the opportunity to pounce on his prey, if he had been seeking prey. But at no time had he shown the desire to harm them.

It may be that the beavers discussed the matter fully among themselves. It is possible that Umisk and his playmates told their parents of their adventure, and of how Baree made no move to harm them when he could quite easily have caught them. It is also more than likely that the older beavers who had fled from Baree that morning gave an account of their adventures, again emphasizing the fact that the stranger, while frightening them, had shown no disposition to attack them. All this is quite possible, for if beavers can make a large part of a continent's history, and can perform

77

engineering feats that nothing less than dynamite can destroy, it is only reasonable to suppose that they have some way of making one another understand.

However this may be, courageous old Beaver-tooth took it upon himself to end the suspense.

It was early in the afternoon that for the third or fourth time Baree walked out on the dam. This dam was fully two hundred feet in length, but at no point did the water run over it, the overflow finding its way through narrow sluices. A week or two ago Baree could have crossed to the opposite side of the pond on this dam, but now—at the far end—Beaver-tooth and his engineers were adding a new section of dam, and in order to accomplish their work more easily, they had flooded fully fifty yards of the low ground on which they were working. The main dam held a fascination for Baree. It was strong with the smell of beaver. The top of it was high and dry, and there were dozens of smoothly worn little hollows in which the beavers had taken their sunbaths. In one of these hollows Baree stretched himself out, with his eyes on the pond. Not a ripple stirred its velvety smoothness. Not a sound broke the drowsy stillness of the afternoon. The beavers might have been dead or asleep, for all the stir they made. And yet they knew that Baree was on the dam. Where he lay, the sun fell in a warm flood, and it was so comfortable that after a time he had difficulty in keeping his eyes open to watch the pond. Then he fell asleep.

Just how Beaver-tooth sensed this fact is a mystery. Five minutes later he came up quietly, without a splash or a sound, within fifty yards of Baree. For a few moments he scarcely moved in the water. Then he swam very slowly parallel with the dam across the pond. At the other side he drew himself ashore, and for another minute sat as motionless as a stone, with his eyes on that part of the dam where Baree was lying. Not another beaver was moving, and it was very soon apparent that Beaver-tooth had but one object in mind—getting a closer observation of Baree. When he entered the water again, he swam along close to the dam. Ten feet beyond Baree he began to climb out. He did this with great slowness and caution. At last he reached the top of the dam.

A few yards away Baree was almost hidden in his hollow, only the top of his shiny black body appearing to Beaver-tooth's scrutiny. To get a better look, the old beaver spread his flat tail out beyond him and rose to a sitting position on his hindquarters, his two front paws held squirrel-like over his breast. In this pose he was fully three feet tall. He probably weighed forty pounds, and in some ways he resembled one of those fat, good-natured, silly-looking dogs that go largely to stomach. But his brain was working with amazing celerity. Suddenly he gave the hard mud of the dam a single slap with his tail—and Baree sat up. Instantly he saw Beaver-tooth, and stared. Beaver-tooth stared. For a full half-minute neither moved the thousandth part of an inch. The Baree stood up and wagged his tail.

That was enough. Dropping to his forefeet, Beaver-tooth waddled leisurely to the edge of the dam and dived over. He was neither cautious nor in very great haste now. He made a great commotion in the water and swam boldly back and forth under Baree. When he had done this several times, he cut straight up the pond to the largest of the three houses and disappeared. Five minutes after Beaver-tooth's exploit, word was passing quickly among the colony. The stranger—Baree—was not a lynx. He was not a fox. He was not a wolf. Moreover, he was very young—and harmless. Work could be resumed. Play could be resumed. There was no danger. Such was Beaver-tooth's verdict.

If someone had shouted these facts in beaver language through a megaphone, the response could not have been quicker. All at once it seemed to Baree, who was still standing on the edge of the dam, that the pond was alive with beavers. He had never seen so many at one time before. They were popping up everywhere, and some of them swam up within a dozen feet of him and looked him over in a leisurely and curious way. For perhaps five minutes the beavers seemed to have no particular object in view. Then Beaver-tooth himself struck straight for the shore and climbed out. Others followed him. Half a dozen workers disappeared in the canals. As many more waddled out among the alders and willows. Eagerly Baree watched for Umisk and his chums. At last he saw them, swimming forth from one of the smaller houses. They climbed out on their playground—the smooth bar above the shore of mud. Baree wagged his tail so hard that his whole body shook, and hurried along the dam.

When he came out on the level strip of shore, Umisk was there alone, nibbling his supper from a long, freshly cut willow. The other little beavers had gone into a thick clump of young alders.

This time Umisk did not run. He looked up from his stick. Baree squatted himself, wiggling in a most friendly and ingratiating manner. For a few seconds Umisk regarded him.

Then, very coolly, he resumed his supper.

CHAPTER X

JUST as in the life of every man there is one big, controlling influence, either for good or bad, so in the life of Baree the beaver pond was largely an arbiter of destiny. Where he might have gone if he had not discovered it, and what might have happened to him, are matters of conjecture. But it held him. It began to take the place of the old windfall, and in the beavers themselves he found a companionship which made up, in a way, for his loss of the protection and friendship of Kazan and Gray Wolf.

This companionship, if it could be called that, went just so far and no farther. With each day that passed the older beavers became more accustomed to seeing Baree. At the end of two weeks, if Baree had gone away, they would have missed him—but not in the same way that Baree would have missed the beavers. It was a matter of good-natured toleration on their part. With Baree it was different. He was still *uskahis*, as Nepeese would have said; he still wanted mothering; he was still moved by the puppyish yearnings which he had not yet had the time to outgrow; and when night came—to speak that yearning quite plainly—he had the desire to go into the big beaver house with Umisk and his chums and sleep.

During this fortnight that followed Beaver-tooth's exploit on the dam Baree ate his meals a mile up the creek, where there were plenty of crayfish. But the pond was home. Night always found him there, and a large part of his day. He slept at the end of the dam, or on top of it on particularly clear nights, and the beavers accepted him as a permanent guest. They worked in his presence as if he did not exist.

Baree was fascinated by this work, and he never grew tired of watching it. It puzzled and bewildered him. Day after day he saw them float timber and brush through the water for the new dam. He saw this dam growing steadily under their efforts. One day he lay within a dozen feet of an old beaver who was cutting down a tree six inches through. When the tree fell, and the old beaver scurried away, Baree scurried, too. Then he came back and smelled of the cutting, wondering what it was all about, and why Umisk's uncle or grandfather or aunt had gone to all that trouble.

He still could not induce Umisk and the other young beavers to join him in play, and after the first week or so he gave up his efforts. In fact, their play puzzled him almost as much as the dam-building operations of the older beavers. Umisk, for instance, was fond of playing in the mud at the edge of the pond. He was like a very small boy. Where his elders floated timbers from three inches to a foot in diameter to the big dam, Umisk brought small sticks and twigs no larger around than a lead pencil to his playground, and built a make-believe dam of his own.

Umisk would work an hour at a time on this play dam as industriously as his father and mother were working on the big dam, and Baree would lie flat on his belly a few feet away, watching him and wondering mightily. And through this half-dry mud Umisk would also dig his miniature canals, just as a small boy might have dug his Mississippi River and pirate-infested oceans in the outflow of some back-lot spring. With his sharp little teeth he cut down his big timber— willow sprouts never more than an inch in diameter; and when one of these four- or five-foot sprouts toppled down, he undoubtedly felt as great a satisfaction as Beaver-tooth felt when he sent a seventy-foot birch crashing into the edge of the pond. Baree could not understand the fun of all this. He could see some reason for nibbling at sticks—he liked to sharpen his teeth on sticks himself; but it puzzled him to explain why Umisk so painstakingly stripped the bark from the sticks and swallowed it.

Another method of play still further discouraged Baree's advances. A short distance from the spot where he had first seen Umisk there was a shelving bank that rose ten or twelve feet from the water, and this bank was used by the young beavers as a slide. It was worn smooth and hard. Umisk would climb up the bank at a point where it was not so steep. At the top of the slide he would put his tail out flat behind him and give himself a shove, shooting down the toboggan and landing in the water with a big splash. At times there were from six to ten young beavers engaged in this sport, and now and then one of the older beavers would waddle to the top of the slide and take a turn with the youngsters.

One afternoon, when the toboggan was particularly wet and slippery from recent use, Baree went up the beaver path to the top of the bank, and began investigating. Nowhere had he found the beaver-smell so strong as on the slide. He began sniffing and incautiously went too far. In an instant his feet shot out from under him, and with a single wild yelp he went shooting down the toboggan. For the second time in his life he found himself struggling under water, and when a minute or two later he dragged himself up through the soft mud to the firmer footing of the shore, he had at last a very well-defined opinion of beaver play.

It may be that Umisk saw him. It may be that very soon the story of his adventure was known by all the inhabitants of Beaver Town. For when Baree came upon Umisk eating his supper of alderbark that evening, Umisk stood his ground to the last inch, and for the first time they smelled noses. At least Baree sniffed audibly, and plucky little Umisk sat like a rolled-up sphinx. That was the final cementing of their friendship—on Baree's part. He capered about extravagantly for a few moments, telling Umisk how much he liked him, and that they'd be great chums. Umisk didn't talk. He didn't make a move until he resumed his supper. But he was a companionable-looking little fellow, for all that, and Baree was happier than he had been since the day he left the old windfall.

This friendship, even though it outwardly appeared to be quite one-sided, was decidedly fortunate for Umisk. When Baree was at the pond, he always kept as near to Umisk as possible, when he could find him. One day he was lying in a patch of grass, half asleep, while Umisk busied himself in a clump of alder shoots a few yards away. It was the warning crack of a beaver tail that fully roused Baree; and then another and another, like pistol shots. He jumped up. Everywhere beavers were scurrying for the pond.

Just then Umisk came out of the alders and hurried as fast as his short, fat legs would carry him toward the water. He had almost reached the mud when a lightning flash of red passed before Baree's eyes in the afternoon sun, and in another instant Napakasew— the he-fox—had fastened his sharp fangs in Umisk's throat. Baree heard his little friend's agonized cry; he heard the frenzied *flap-flap-flap* of many tails—and his blood pounded suddenly with the thrill of excitement and rage.

As swiftly as the red fox himself, Baree darted to the rescue. He was as big and as heavy as the fox, and when he struck Napakasew, it was with a ferocious snarl that Pierrot might have heard on the farther side of the pond, and his teeth sank like knives into the shoulder of Umisk's assailant. The fox was of a breed of forest highwaymen which kills from behind. He was not a fighter when it came fang-to-fang, unless cornered—and so fierce and sudden was Baree's assault that Napakasew took to flight almost as quickly as he had begun his attack on Umisk.

Baree did not follow him, but went to Umisk, who lay half in the mud, whimpering and snuffling in a curious sort of way. Gently Baree nosed him, and after a moment or two Umisk got up on his webbed feet, while fully twenty or thirty beavers were making a tremendous fuss in the water near the shore.

After this the beaver pond seemed more than ever like home to Baree.

CHAPTER XI

WHILE lovely Nepeese was shuddering over her thrilling experience under the rock— while Pierrot still offered grateful thanks in his prayers for her deliverance and Baree was becoming more and more a fixture at the beaver pond—Bush McTaggart was perfecting a little scheme of his own up at Post Lac Bain, about forty miles north and west. McTaggart had been factor at Lac Bain for seven years. In the company's books down in Winnipeg he was counted a remarkably successful man. The expense of his post was below the average, and his semi-annual report of furs always ranked among the first. After his name, kept on file in the main office, was one notation which said: "Gets more out of a dollar than any other man north of God's Lake."

The Indians knew why this was so. They called him *Napao Wetikoo*—the man-devil. This was under their breath—a name whispered sinisterly in the glow of tepee fires, or spoken softly where not even the winds might carry it to the ears of Bush McTaggart. They feared him; they hated him. They died of starvation and sickness, and the tighter Bush McTaggart clenched the fingers of his iron rule, the more meekly, it seemed to him, did they respond to his mastery. His was a small soul, hidden in the hulk of a brute, which rejoiced in power. And here—with the raw wilderness on four sides of him—his power knew no end. The Big Company was behind him. It had made him king of a domain in which there was little law except his own. And in return he gave back to the company bales and bundles of furs beyond their expectation. It was not for them to have suspicions. They were a thousand or more miles away—and dollars counted.

Gregson might have told. Gregson was the Investigating Agent of that district, who visited McTaggart once each year. He might have reported that the Indians called McTaggart *Napao Wetikoo* because he gave them only half-price for their furs; he might have told the company quite plainly that he kept the people of the traplines at the edge of starvation through every month of the winter, that he had them on their knees with his hands at their throats—putting the truth in a mild and pretty way—and that he always had a woman or a girl, Indian or halfbreed, living with him at the Post. But Gregson enjoyed his visits too much at Lac Bain. Always he could count on two weeks of coarse pleasures; and in addition to that, his own womenfolk at home wore a rich treasure of fur that came to them from McTaggart.

One evening, a week after the adventure of Nepeese and Baree under the rock, McTaggart sat under the glow of an oil lamp in his "store." He had sent his little pippin-faced English clerk to bed, and he was alone. For six weeks there had been in him a great unrest. It was just six weeks ago that Pierrot had brought Nepeese on her first visit to Lac Bain since McTaggart had been factor there. She had taken his breath away. Since then he had been able to think of nothing but her. Twice in that six weeks he had gone down to Pierrot's cabin. Tomorrow he was going again. Marie, the slim Cree girl over in his cabin, he had forgotten—just as a dozen others before Marie had slipped out of his memory. It was Nepeese now. He had never seen anything quite so beautiful as Pierrot's girl.

Audibly he cursed Pierrot as he looked at a sheet of paper under his hand, on which for an hour or more he had been making notes out of worn and dusty company ledgers. It was Pierrot who stood in his way. Pierrot's father, according to those notes, had been a full-blooded Frenchman. Therefore Pierrot was half French, and Nepeese was quarter French—though she was so beautiful he could have sworn there was not more than a drop or two of Indian blood in her veins. If they had been all Indian—Chippewayan, Cree, Ojibway, Dog Rib—anything—there would have been no trouble at all in the matter. He would have bent them to his power, and Nepeese would have come to his cabin, as Marie came six months ago. But there was the accursed French of it! Pierrot and Nepeese were different. And yet—

He smiled grimly, and his hands clenched tighter. After all, was not his power sufficient? Would even Pierrot dare stand against that? If Pierrot objected, he would drive him from the country—from the trapping regions that had come down to him as heritage from father and grandfather, and even before their day. He would make of Pierrot a wanderer and an outcast, as he had made wanderers and outcasts of a score of others who had lost his favor. No other post would sell to or buy from Pierrot if *La Bête*—the black cross— was put after his name. That was his power—a law of the Factors that had come down through the centuries. It was a tremendous power for evil. It had brought him Marie, the slim, dark-eyed Cree girl, who hated him—and in spite of her hatred "kept house for him." That was the polite way of explaining her presence if explanations were ever necessary.

McTaggart looked again at the notes he had made on the sheet of paper. Pierrot's trapping country, his own property according to the common law of the wilderness, was very valuable. During the last seven years he had received an average of a thousand dollars a year for his furs, for McTaggart had been unable to cheat Pierrot quite as completely as he had cheated the Indians. A thousand dollars a year! Pierrot would think twice before he gave that up. McTaggart chuckled as he crumpled the paper in his hand and prepared to put out the light. Under his close-cropped shaggy beard his reddish face glazed with the fire that was in his blood. It was an unpleasant face—like iron, merciless, filled with the look that gave him his name of *Napao Wetikoo*. His eyes gleamed, and he drew a quick breath as he put out the light.

He chuckled again as he made his way through the darkness to the door. Nepeese as good as belonged to him. He would have her if it cost—*Pierrot's life*. And—*why not?* It was all so easy. A shot on a lonely trapline, a single knife thrust—and who would know? Who would guess where Pierrot had gone? And it would all be Pierrot's fault. For the last time he had seen Pierrot, he had made an honest proposition: he would marry Nepeese. Yes, even that. He had told Pierrot so. He had told Pierrot that when the latter was his father-in-law, he would pay him double price for furs.

And Pierrot had stared—had stared with that strange, stunned look in his face, like a man dazed by a blow from a club. And so if he did not get Nepeese without trouble it would all be Pierrot's fault. Tomorrow McTaggart would start again for the halfbreed's country. And the next day Pierrot would have an answer for him. Bush McTaggart chuckled again when he went to bed.

Until the next to the last day Pierrot said nothing to Nepeese about what had passed between him and the Factor at Lac Bain. Then he told her.

"He is a beast—a man-devil," he said, when he had finished. "I would rather see you out there—with her—dead." And he pointed to the tall spruce under which the princess-mother lay.

Nepeese had not uttered a sound. But her eyes had grown bigger and darker, and there was a flush in her cheeks which Pierrot had never seen there before. She stood up when he had done, and she seemed taller to him. Never had she looked quite so much like a woman, and Pierrot's eyes were deep-shadowed with fear and uneasiness as he watched her while she gazed off into the northwest—toward Lac Bain.

She was wonderful, this slip of a girl-woman. Her beauty troubled him. He had seen the look in Bush McTaggart's eyes. He had heard the thrill in Mc-Taggart's voice. He had caught the desire of a beast in McTaggart's face. It had frightened him at first. But now—he was not frightened. He was uneasy, but his hands were clenched. In his heart there was a smoldering fire. At last Nepeese turned and came and sat down beside him again, at his feet.

"He is coming tomorrow, *ma chérie*," he said. "What shall I tell him?"

The Willow's lips were red. Her eyes shone. But she did not look up at her father.

"Nothing, Nootawe—except that you are to say to him that I am the one to whom he must come—for what he seeks."

Pierrot bent over and caught her smiling. The sun went down. His heart sank with it, like cold lead.

From Lac Bain to Pierrot's cabin the trail cut within half a mile of the beaver pond, a dozen miles from where Pierrot lived; and it was here, on a twist of the creek in which Wakayoo had caught fish for Baree, that Bush McTaggart made his camp for the night. Only twenty miles of the journey could be made by canoe, and as McTaggart was traveling the last stretch afoot, his camp was a simple affair—a few cut balsams, a light blanket, a small fire. Before he prepared his supper, the Factor drew a number of copper-wire snares from his small pack and spent half an hour in setting them in rabbit runways. This method of securing meat was far less arduous than carrying a gun in hot weather, and it was certain. Half a dozen snares were good for at least three rabbits, and one of these three was sure to be young and tender enough for the frying pan. After he had placed his snares, McTaggart set a skillet of bacon over the coals and boiled his coffee.

Of all the odors of a camp, the smell of bacon reaches farthest in the forest. It needs no wind. It drifts on its own wings. On a still night a fox will sniff it a mile away—twice that far if the air is moving in the right direction. It was this smell of bacon that came to Baree where he lay in his hollow on top of the beaver dam.

Since his experience in the canyon and the death of Wakayoo, he had not fared particularly well. Caution had held him near the pond, and he had lived almost entirely on crayfish. This new perfume that came with the night wind roused his hunger. But it was elusive: now he could smell it—the next instant it was gone. He left the dam and began questing for the source of it in the forest, until after a time he lost it altogether. McTaggart had finished frying his bacon and was eating it.

It was a splendid night that followed. Perhaps Baree would have slept through it in his nest on the top of the dam if the bacon smell had not stirred the new hunger in him. Since his adventure in the canyon, the deeper forest had held a dread for him, especially at night. But this night was like a pale, golden day: it was moonless; but the stars shone like a billion distant lamps, flooding the world in a soft and billowy sea of light. A gentle whisper of wind made pleasant sounds in the treetops. Beyond that it was very quiet, for it was *Puskowepesim*—the Moulting Moon—and the wolves were not hunting, the owls had lost their voice, the foxes slunk with the silence of shadows, and even the beavers had begun to cease their labors. The horns of the moose, the deer, and the caribou were in tender velvet, and they moved but little and fought not at all. It was late July, Moulting Moon of the Cree, Moon of Silence for the Chippewayan.

In this silence Baree began to hunt. He stirred up a family of half-grown partridges, but they escaped him. He pursued a rabbit that was swifter than he. For an hour he had no luck. Then he heard a sound that made every drop of blood in him thrill. He was close to McTaggart's camp, and what he had heard was a rabbit in one of McTaggart's snares. He came out into a little starlit open and there he saw the rabbit going through a most marvelous pantomime. It amazed him for a moment, and he stopped in his tracks.

Wapoos, the rabbit, had run his furry head into the snare, and his first frightened jump had "shot" the sapling to which the copper wire was attached so that he was now hung half in midair, with only his hind feet touching the ground. And there he was dancing madly while the noose about his neck slowly choked him to death.

Baree gave a sort of gasp. He could understand nothing of the part that the wire and the sapling were playing in this curious game. All he could see was that Wapoos was hopping and dancing about on his hind legs in a most puzzling and unrabbit-like fashion. It may be that he thought it some sort of play. In this instance, however, he did not regard Wapoos as he had looked on Umisk the beaver. He knew that Wapoos made mighty fine eating, and after another moment or two of hesitation he darted upon his prey.

Wapoos, half gone already, made almost no struggle, and in the glow of the stars Baree finished him, and for half an hour afterward he feasted.

McTaggart had heard no sound, for the snare into which Wapoos had run his head was the one set farthest from his camp. Beside the smoldering coals of his fire he sat with his back to a tree, smoking his black pipe and dreaming covetously of Nepeese, when Baree continued his night-wandering. Baree no longer had the desire to hunt. He was too full. But he nosed in and out of the starlit spaces, enjoying immensely the stillness and the golden glow of the night. He was following a rabbit run when he came to a place where two fallen logs left a trail no wider than his body. He squeezed through; something tightened about his neck; there was a sudden snap—a swish as the sapling was released from its "trigger"—and Baree was jerked off his feet so suddenly that he had no time to conjecture as to what was happening.

The yelp in his throat died in a gurgle, and the next moment he was going through the pantomimic actions of Wapoos, who was having his vengeance inside him. For the life of him Baree could not keep from dancing about, while the wire grew tighter and tighter about his neck. When he snapped at the wire and flung the weight of his body to the ground, the sapling would bend obligingly, and then—in its rebound—would yank him for an instant completely off the earth. Furiously he struggled. It was a miracle that the fine wire held him. In a few moments more it must have broken—but McTaggart had heard him! The Factor caught up his blanket and a heavy stick as he hurried toward the snare. It was not a rabbit making those sounds—he knew that. Perhaps a fisher cat—a lynx, a fox, a young wolf—

It was the wolf he thought of first when he saw Baree at the end of the wire. He dropped the blanket and raised the club. If there had been clouds overhead, or the stars had been less brilliant, Baree would have died as surely as Wapoos had died. With the club raised over his head McTaggart saw in time the white star, the white-tipped ear, and the jet black of Baree's coat.

With a swift movement he exchanged the club for the blanket.

In that hour, could McTaggart have looked ahead to the days that were to come, he would have used the club. Could he have foreseen the great tragedy in which Baree was to play a vital part, wrecking his hopes and destroying his world, he would have beaten him to a pulp there under the light of the stars. And Baree, could he have foreseen what was to happen between this brute with a white skin and the most beautiful thing in the forests, would have fought even more bitterly before he surrendered himself to the smothering embrace of the Factor's blanket. On this night Fate had played a strange hand for them both, and only that Fate, and perhaps the stars above, held a knowledge of what its outcome was to be.

CHAPTER XII

HALF an hour later Bush McTaggart's fire was burning brightly again. In the glow of it Baree lay trussed up like an Indian papoose, tied into a balloon-shaped ball with *babiche* thong, his head alone showing where his captor had cut a hole for it in the blanket. He was hopelessly caught—so closely imprisoned in the blanket that he could scarcely move a muscle of his body. A few feet away from him McTaggart was bathing a bleeding hand in a basin of water. There was also a red streak down the side of McTaggart's bullish neck.

"You little devil!" he snarled at Baree. "You little devil!"

He reached over suddenly and gave Baree's head a vicious blow with his heavy hand.

"I ought to beat your brains out, and—I believe I will!"

Baree watched him as he picked up a stick close at his side—a bit of firewood. Pierrot had chased him, but this was the first time he had been near enough to the man-monster to see the red glow in his eyes. They were not like the eyes of the wonderful creature who had almost caught him in the web of her hair, and who had crawled after him under the rock. They were beast eyes. They made him shrink and try to draw his head back into the blanket as the stick was raised. At the same time he snarled. His white fangs gleamed in the firelight. His ears were flat. He wanted to sink his teeth in the red throat where he had already drawn blood.

The stick fell. It fell again and again, and when McTaggart was done, Baree lay half stunned, his eyes partly closed by the blows, and his mouth bleeding.

"That's the way we take the devil out of a wild dog," snarled McTaggart. "I guess you won't try the biting game again, eh, youngster? A thousand devils—but you went almost to the bone of this hand!"

He began washing the wound again. Baree's teeth had sunk deep, and there was a troubled look in the Factor's face. It was July—a bad month for bites. From his kit he got a small flask of whisky and turned a bit of the raw liquor on the wound, cursing Baree as it burned into his flesh.

Baree's half-shut eyes were fixed on him steadily. He knew that at last he had met the deadliest of all his enemies. And yet he was not afraid. The club in Bush McTaggart's hand had not killed his spirit. It had killed his fear. It had roused in him a hatred such as he had never known—not even when he was fighting Ooh-oomisew, the outlaw owl. The vengeful animosity of the wolf was burning in him now, along with the savage courage of the dog. He did not flinch when McTaggart approached him again. He made an effort to raise himself, that he might spring at this man-monster. In the effort, swaddled as he was in the blanket, he rolled over in a helpless and ludicrous heap.

The sight of it touched McTaggart's risibilities, and he laughed. He sat down with his back to the tree again and filled his pipe.

Baree did not take his eyes from McTaggart as he smoked. He watched the man when the latter stretched himself out on the bare ground and went to sleep. He listened, still later, to the man-monster's heinous snoring. Again and again during the long night he struggled to free himself. He would never forget that night. It was terrible. In the thick, hot folds of the blanket his limbs and body were suffocated until the blood almost stood still in his veins. Yet he did not whine.

They began to journey before the sun was up, for if Baree's blood was almost dead within him, Bush McTaggart's was scorching his body with the heat of its anticipation. He made his last plans as he walked swiftly through the forest with Baree under his arm. He would send Pierrot at once for Father Grotin at his mission seventy miles to the west. He would marry Nepeese—yes, marry her! That would tickle Pierrot. And he would be alone with Nepeese while Pierrot was gone for the missioner.

This thought flamed McTaggart's blood like strong whisky. There was no thought in his hot and unreasoning brain of what Nepeese might say—of what she might think. He was not after the soul of her. His hand clenched, and he laughed harshly as there flashed on him for an instant the thought that perhaps Pierrot would not want to give her up. Pierrot! Bah! It would not be the first time he had killed a man—or the second.

McTaggart laughed again, and he walked still faster. There was no chance of his losing—no chance for Nepeese to get away from him. He—Bush McTaggart—was lord of this wilderness, master of its people, arbiter of their destinies. He was power—and the law.

The sun was well up when Pierrot, standing in front of his cabin with Nepeese, pointed to a rise in the trail three or four hundred yards away, over which McTaggart had just appeared.

"He is coming."

With a face which had aged since last night he looked at Nepeese. Again he saw the dark glow in her eyes and the deepening red of her parted lips, and his heart was sick again with dread. Was it possible—

She turned on him, her eyes shining, her voice trembling.

"Remember, Nootawe—you must send him to me for his answer," she cried quickly, and she darted into the cabin. With a cold, gray face Pierrot faced Bush McTaggart.

CHAPTER XIII

FROM the window, her face screened by the folds of the curtain which she had made for it, the Willow saw what happened outside. She was not smiling now. She was breathing quickly, and her body was tense. Bush McTaggart paused not a dozen feet from the window and shook hands with Pierrot, her father. She heard McTaggart's coarse voice, his boisterous greeting, and then she saw him showing Pierrot what he carried under his arm. There came to her distinctly his explanation of how he had caught his captive in a rabbit snare. He unwrapped the blanket. Nepeese gave a cry of amazement. In an instant she was out beside them. She did not look at

McTaggart's red face, blazing in its joy and exultation.

"It is Baree!" she cried.

She took the bundle from McTaggart and turned to Pierrot.

"Tell him that Baree belongs to me," she said.

She hurried into the cabin. McTaggart looked after her, stunned and amazed. Then he looked at Pierrot. A man half blind could have seen that Pierrot was as amazed as he. Nepeese had not spoken to him—the Factor of Lac Bain! She had not *looked* at him! And she had taken the dog from him with as little concern as though he had been a wooden man. The red in his face deepened as he stared from Pierrot to the door through which she had gone, and which she had closed behind her.

On the floor of the cabin Nepeese dropped on her knees and finished unwrapping the blanket. She was not afraid of Baree. She had forgotten McTaggart. And then, as Baree rolled in a limp heap on the floor, she saw his half-closed eyes and the dry blood on his jaws, and the light left her face as swiftly as the sun is shadowed by a cloud.

"Baree," she cried softly. "Baree—Baree!"

She partly lifted him in her two hands. Baree's head sagged. His body was numbed until he was powerless to move. His legs were without feeling. He could scarcely see. But he heard her voice! It was the same voice that had come to him that day he had felt the sting of the bullet, the voice that had pleaded with him under the rock!

The voice of the Willow thrilled Baree. It seemed to

stir the sluggish blood in his veins, and he opened his eyes wider and saw again the wonderful stars that had glowed at him so softly the day of Wakayoo's death. One of the Willow's long braids fell over her shoulder, and he smelled again the sweet scent of her hair as her hand caressed him and her voice talked to him. Then she got up suddenly and left him, and he did not move while he waited for her. In a moment she was back with a basin of water and a cloth. Gently she washed the blood from his eyes and mouth. And still Baree made no move. He scarcely breathed. But Nepeese saw the little quivers that shot through his body when her hand touched him, like electric shocks.

"He beat you with a club," she was saying, her dark eyes within a foot of Baree's. "He beat you! That man-beast!"

There came an interruption. The door opened, and the man-beast stood looking down on them, a grin on his red face. Instantly Baree showed that he was alive. He sprang from under the Willow's hand with a sudden snarl and faced McTaggart. The hair of his spine stood up like a brush; his fangs gleamed menacingly, and his eyes burned like living coals.

"There is a devil in him," said McTaggart. "He is wild—born of the wolf. You must be careful or he will take off a hand, *ka sakahet*!" It was the first time he had called her that lover's name in Cree—*sweetheart*! Her heart pounded. She bent her head for a moment over her clenched hands, and McTaggart—looking down on what he thought was her confusion—laid his hand caressingly on her hair. From the door Pierrot had heard the word, and now he saw the caress, and he raised a hand as if to shut out the sight of a sacrilege.

"*Mon Dieu!*" he breathed.

In the next instant he had given a sharp cry of wonder that mingled with a sudden yell of pain from McTaggart. Like a flash Baree had darted across the floor and fastened his teeth in the Factor's leg. They had bitten deep before McTaggart freed himself with a powerful kick. With an oath he snatched his revolver from its holster. The Willow was ahead of him. With a little cry she darted to Baree and caught him in her arms. As she looked up at McTaggart, her soft, bare throat was within a few inches of Baree's naked fangs. Her eyes blazed.

"You beat him!" she cried. "He hates you—hates you—"

"Let him go!" called Pierrot in an agony of fear.

"*Mon Dieu!* I say let him go or he will tear the life from you!"

"He hates you—hates you—hates you—" the Willow was repeating over and over again into McTaggart's startled face. Then suddenly she turned to her father. "No, he will not tear the life from me," she cried. "See! It is Baree. Did I not tell you that? It is Baree! Is it not proof that he defended me—"

"From me!" gasped McTaggart, his face darkening.

Pierrot advanced and laid a hand on McTaggart's arm. He was smiling.

"Let us leave them to fight it out between themselves, *m'sieu*," he said. "They are two little firebrands, and we are not safe. If she is bitten—"

He shrugged his shoulders. A great load had been lifted from them suddenly. His voice was soft and persuasive. And now the anger had gone out of the Willow's face. A coquettish uplift of her eyes caught McTaggart, and she looked straight at him half smiling, as she spoke to her father.

"I will join you soon, *mon père*—you and *M'sieu* the Factor from Lac Bain!"

There were undeniable little devils in her eyes, McTaggart thought—little devils laughing full at him as she spoke, setting his brain afire and his blood to running wildly. Those eyes—full of dancing witches! How he would tame them and play with them—very soon now! He followed Pierrot outside. In his exultation he no longer felt the smart of Baree's teeth.

"I will show you my new cariole that I have made for winter, *M'sieu*," said Pierrot as the door closed behind them.

Half an hour later Nepeese came out of the cabin. She could see that Pierrot and the Factor had been talking about something that had not been pleasant to her father. His face was strained. She caught in his eyes the smoulder of fire which he was trying to smother, as one might smother flames under a blanket. McTaggart's jaws were set, but his eyes flared up with pleasure when he saw her. She knew what it was about. The Factor from Lac Bain had been demanding his answer of Pierrot, and Pierrot had been telling him what she had insisted upon—that he must come to her. And he was coming! She turned with a quick beating of the heart and hurried down a little path. She heard McTaggart's footsteps behind her, and threw the flash of a smile over her shoulder. But her teeth were set tight. The nails of her fingers were cutting into the palms of her hands.

Pierrot stood without moving. He watched them as they disappeared into the edge of the forest, Nepeese still a few steps ahead of McTaggart. Out of his breast rose a sharp breath.

"Par les mille cornes du diable!" he swore softly. "Is it possible—that she smiles from her heart at that beast? *Non!* It is impossible. And yet—if it is so—"

One of his brown hands tightened convulsively about the handle of the knife in his belt, and slowly he began to follow them.

McTaggart did not hurry to overtake Nepeese. She was following the narrow path deeper into the forest, and he was glad of that. They would be alone—away from Pierrot. He was ten steps behind her, and again the Willow smiled at him over her shoulder. Her body moved sinuously and swiftly. She was keeping accurate measurement of the distance between them—but McTaggart did not guess that this was why she looked back every now and then. He was satisfied to let her go on. When she turned from the narrow trail into a side path that scarcely bore the mark of travel, his heart gave an exultant jump. If she kept on, he would very soon have her alone—a good distance from the cabin. The blood ran hot in his face. He did not speak to her, through fear that she would stop. Ahead of them he heard the rumble of water. It was the creek running through the chasm.

Nepeese was making straight for that sound. With a little laugh she started to run, and when she stood at the edge of the chasm, McTaggart was fully fifty yards behind her. Twenty feet sheer down there was a deep pool between the rock walls, a pool so deep that it was like blue ink. She turned to face the Factor from Lac Bain. He had never looked more like a red beast to her. Until this moment she had been unafraid. But now—in an instant—he terrified her Before she could speak what she had planned to say, he was at her side, and had taken her face between his two great hands, his coarse fingers twining in the silken strands of her thick braids where they fell over her shoulders at the neck.

"*Ka sakahet!*" he cried passionately. "Pierrot said you would have an answer for me. But I need no answer now. You are mine! Mine!"

She gave a cry. It was a gasping, broken cry. His arms were about her like bands of iron, crushing her slender body, shutting off her breath, turning the world almost black for her. She could neither struggle nor cry out. She felt the hot passion of his lips on her face, heard his voice—and then came a moment's freedom, and air into her strangled lungs. Pierrot was calling! He had come to the fork in the trail, and he was calling the Willow's name!

McTaggart's hot hand came over her mouth.

"Don't answer," she heard him say.

Strength—anger—hatred flared up in her, and fiercely she struck the hand down. Something in her wonderful eyes held McTaggart. They blazed into his very soul.

"*Bête noire!*" she panted at him, freeing herself from the last touch of his hands. "Beast—black beast!" Her voice trembled, and her face flamed. "See—I came to show you my pool—and tell you what you wanted to hear—and you—you—have crushed me like a beast— like a great rock— See! down there—it is my pool!"

She had not planned it like this. She had intended to be smiling, even laughing, in this moment. But McTaggart had spoiled them—her carefully made plans! And yet, as she pointed, the Factor from Lac Bain looked for an instant over the edge of the chasm. And then she laughed—laughed as she gave him a sudden shove from behind.

"And that is my answer, *M'sieu le Facteur* from Lac Bain!" she cried tauntingly as he plunged headlong into the deep pool between the rock walls.

CHAPTER XIV

FROM the edge of the open Pierrot saw what had happened, and he gave a great gasp. He drew back among the balsams. This was not a moment for him to show himself. While his heart drummed like a hammer, his face was filled with joy.

On her hands and knees the Willow was peering over the edge. Bush McTaggart had disappeared. He had gone down like the great clod he was; the water of her pool had closed over him with a dull splash that was like a chuckle of triumph. He appeared now, beating out with his arms and legs to keep himself afloat, while the Willow's voice came to him in taunting cries.

"*Bête noire! Bête noire!* Beast! Beast—"

She flung small sticks and tufts of earth down at him fiercely; and McTaggart, looking up as he gained his equilibrium, saw her leaning so far over that she seemed about to fall. Her long braids hung down into the chasm, gleaming in the sun; her eyes were laughing while her lips taunted him; he could see the flash of her white teeth.

"Beast! Beast!"

He began swimming, still looking up at her. It was a hundred yards down the slow-going current to the beach of shale where he could climb out, and a half of that distance she followed him, laughing and taunting him, and flinging down sticks and pebbles. He noted that none of the sticks or stones was large enough to hurt him. When at last his feet touched bottom, she was gone.

Swiftly Nepeese ran back over the trail, and almost into Pierrot's arms. She was panting and laughing when for a moment she stopped.

"I have given him the answer, Nootawe! He is in the pool!"

Into the balsams she disappeared like a bird. Pierrot made no effort to stop her or to follow.

"*Tonnerre de Dieu!*" he chuckled—and cut straight across for the other trail.

* * *

Nepeese was out of breath when she reached the cabin. Baree, fastened to a table leg by a *babiche* thong, heard her pause for a moment at the door. Then she entered and came straight to him. During the half-hour of her absence Baree had scarcely moved. That half-hour, and the few minutes that had proceeded it, had made tremendous impressions upon him. Nature, heredity, and instinct were at work, clashing and read-justing, impinging on him a new intelligence—the beginning of a new understanding. A swift and savage impulse had made him leap at Bush McTaggart when the Factor put his hand on the Willow's head. It was not reason. It was a hearkening back of the dog to that day long ago when Kazan, his father, had killed the man-brute in the tent, the man-brute who had dared to attempt the sacrilege of Thorpe's wife, whom Kazan worshiped. It was the dog—and woman.

And here again it was the woman. She had called to the great hidden passion that was in Baree and that had come to him from Kazan. Of all the living things in the world, he knew that he must not hurt this crea-ture that appeared to him through the door. He trem-bled as she knelt before him again, and up through the years came the wild and glorious surge of Kazan's blood, overwhelming the wolf, submerging the sav-agery of his birth—and with his head flat on the floor he whined softly, and *wagged his tail*.

Nepeese gave a cry of joy.

"Baree!" she whispered, taking his head in her hands. "Baree!"

Her touch thrilled him. It sent little throbs through

his body, a tremulous quivering which she could feel and which deepened the glow in her eyes. Gently her hand stroked his head and his back. It seemed to Nepeese that he did not breathe. Under the caress of her hand his eyes closed. In another moment she was talking to him, and at the sound of her voice his eyes shot open.

"He will come here—that beast—and he will kill us," she was saying. "He will kill you because you bit him, Baree. Ugh, I wish you were bigger, and stronger, so that you could take off his head for me!"

She was untying the *babiche* from about the table leg, and under her breath she laughed. She was not frightened. It was a tremendous adventure—and she throbbed with exultation at the thought of having beaten the man-beast in her own way. She could see him in the pool struggling and beating about like a great fish. He was just about crawling out of the chasm now—and she laughed again as she caught Baree up under her arm.

"Oh—*oopi-nao*—but you are heavy!" she gasped. "And yet I must carry you—because I am going to run!"

She hurried outside. Pierrot had not come, and she darted swiftly into the balsams back of the cabin, with Baree hung in the crook of her arm, like a sack filled at both ends and tied in the middle. He felt like that, too. But he still had no inclination to wriggle himself free. Nepeese ran with him until her arm ached. Then she stopped and put him down on his feet, holding to the end of the caribou skin thong that was tied about his neck. She was prepared for any lunge he might make to escape. She expected that he would make an attempt, and for a few moments she watched him closely, while Baree, with his feet on earth once more, looked about him. And then the Willow spoke to him softly.

"You are not going to run away, Baree. *Non*, you are going to stay with me, and we will kill that man-beast if he dares do to me again what he did back there." She flung back the loose hair from about her flushed face, and for a moment she forgot Baree as she thought of that half-minute at the edge of the chasm. He was looking straight up at her when her glance fell on him again. "*Non*, you are not going to run away—you are going to follow me," she whispered. "Come."

The *babiche* string tightened about Baree's neck as she urged him to follow. It was like another rabbit snare, and he braced his forefeet and bared his fangs just a little. The Willow did not pull. Fearlessly she put her hand on his head again. From the direction of the cabin came a shout, and at the sound of it she took Baree up under her arm once more.

"*Bête noire—bête noire!*" she called back tauntingly, but only loud enough to be heard a few yards away. "Go back to Lac Bain—*owases*—you wild beast!"

Nepeese began to make her way swiftly through the forest. It grew deeper and darker, and there were no trails. Three times in the next half-hour she stopped to put Baree down and rest her arm. Each time she pleaded with him coaxingly to follow her. The second and third times Baree wriggled and wagged his tail, but beyond those demonstrations of his satisfaction at the turn his affairs had taken he would not go. When the string tightened around his neck, he braced himself; once he growled—again he snapped viciously at the *babiche*. So Nepeese continued to carry him.

They came at last into an open. It was a tiny meadow in the heart of the forest, not more than three or four times as big as the cabin; underfoot the grass was soft and green, and thick with flowers. Straight through the heart of this little oasis trickled a streamlet across which the Willow jumped with Baree under her arm, and on the edge of the rill was a small wigwam made of freshly cut spruce and balsam boughs. Into her diminutive *mekewap* the Willow thrust her head to see that things were as she had left them yesterday. Then, with a long breath of relief, she put down her four-legged burden and fastened the end of the *babiche* to one of the cut spruce limbs.

Baree burrowed himself back into the wall of the wigwam, and with head alert—and eyes wide open—watched attentively what happened after this. Not a movement of the Willow escaped him. She was radiant—and happy. Her laugh, sweet and wild as a bird's trill, set Baree's heart throbbing with a desire to jump about with her among the flowers.

For a time Nepeese seemed to forget Baree. Her wild blood raced with the joy of her triumph over the Factor from Lac Bain. She saw him again, floundering about in the pool—pictured him at the cabin now, soaked and angry, demanding of *mon père* where she had gone. And *mon père*, with a shrug of his shoulders, was telling him that he didn't know—that probably she had run off into the forest. It did not enter into her head that in tricking Bush McTaggart in that way she had played with dynamite. She did not foresee the peril that in an instant would have stamped the wild flush from her face and curdled the blood in her veins—did not guess that McTaggart had become for her a deadlier menace than ever.

Nepeese knew that he was angry. But what had she to fear? *Mon père* would be angry, too, if she told him what had happened at the edge of the chasm. But she would not tell him. He might kill the beast from Lac Bain. A factor was great. But Pierrot, her father, was greater. It was an unlimited faith in her, born of her mother. Perhaps even now Pierrot was sending him back to Lac Bain, telling him that his business was there. But she would not return to the cabin to see. She would wait here. *Mon père* would understand— and he knew where to find her when the beast was gone. But it would have been such fun to throw sticks at him as he went!

After a little, Nepeese returned to Baree. She brought him water and gave him a piece of raw fish. For hours they were alone, and with each hour there grew stronger in Baree the desire to follow the girl in every movement she made, to crawl close to her when she sat down, to feel the touch of her dress, of her hand—and hear her voice. But he did not show this desire. He was still a little savage of the forests—a four-footed barbarian born half of a wolf and half of a dog; and he lay still. With Umisk he would have played. With Oohoomisew he would have fought. At Bush McTaggart he would have bared his fangs, and buried them deep when the chance came. But the girl was different. Like the Kazan of old, he had begun to worship. If the Willow had freed Baree, he would not have run away. If she had left him, he would possibly have followed her—at a distance. His eyes were never away from her. He watched her build a small fire and cook a piece of the fish. He watched her eat her dinner. It was quite late in the afternoon when she came and sat down close to him, with her lap full of flowers which she twined in the long, shining braids of her hair. Then, playfully, she began beating Baree with the end of one of these braids. He shrank under the soft blows, and with that low, birdlike laughter in her throat, Nepeese drew his head into her lap, where the scatter of flowers lay. She talked to him. Her hand stroked his head. Then it remained still, so near that he wanted to thrust out his warm red tongue and caress it. He breathed in the flower-scented perfume of it—and lay as if dead. It was a glorious moment. Nepeese, looking down on him, could not see that he was breathing.

There came an interruption. It was the snapping of a dry stick. Through the forest Pierrot had come with the stealth of a cat, and when they looked up, he stood at the edge of the open. Baree knew that it was not Bush McTaggart. But it was a man-beast! Instantly his body stiffened under the Willow's hand. He drew back slowly and cautiously from her lap, and as Pierrot advanced, Baree snarled. The next instant Nepeese had risen and had run to Pierrot. The look in her father's face alarmed her.

"What has happened, *mon père*?" she cried.

Pierrot shrugged his shoulders.

"Nothing, *ma Nepeese*—except that you have roused a thousand devils in the heart of the Factor from Lac Bain, and that—"

He stopped as he saw Baree, and pointed at him.

"Last night when *M'sieu* the Factor caught him in a snare, he bit *M'sieu*'s hand. *M'sieu*'s hand is swollen twice its size, and I can see his blood turning black. It is *pechipoo*."

"*Pechipoo*?" gasped Nepeese.

She looked into Pierrot's eyes. They were dark, and filled with a sinister gleam—a flash of exultation, she thought.

"Yes, it is the blood poison," said Pierrot. A gleam of cunning shot into his eyes as he looked over his shoulder, and nodded. "I have hidden the medicine—and told him there is no time to lose in getting back to Lac Bain. And he is afraid—that devil! He is waiting. With that blackening hand, he is afraid to start back alone—and so I go with him. And—listen, *ma Nepeese*. We will be away by sundown, and there is something you must know before I go."

Baree saw them there, close together in the shadows thrown by the tall spruce trees. He heard the low murmur of their voices—chiefly of Pierrot's—and at last he saw Nepeese put her two arms up around the man-beast's neck, and then Pierrot went away again into the forest. He thought that the Willow would never turn her face toward him after that. For a long time she stood looking in the direction which Pierrot had taken. And when after a time she turned and came back to Baree, she did not look like the Nepeese who had been twining flowers in her hair. The laughter was gone from her face and eyes. She knelt down beside him and with sudden fierceness she cried:

"It is *pechipoo*, Baree! It was you—you—who put the poison in his blood. And I hope he dies! For I am afraid—afraid!"

She shivered.

Perhaps it was in this moment that the Great Spirit of things meant Baree to understand—that at last it was given him to comprehend that his day had dawned, that the rising and the setting of his sun no longer existed in the sky but in this girl whose hand rested on his head. He whined softly, and inch by inch he dragged himself nearer to her until again his head rested in the hollow of her lap.

CHAPTER XV

FOR a long time after Pierrot left them the Willow did not move from where she had seated herself beside Baree. It was at last the deepening shadows and a near rumble in the sky that roused her from the fear of the things Pierrot had told her. When she looked up, black clouds were massing slowly over the open space above the spruce-tops. Darkness was falling. In the whisper of the wind and the dead stillness of the thickening gloom there was the sullen brewing of storm. Tonight there would be no glorious sunset. There would be no twilight hour in which to follow the trail, no moon, no stars—and unless Pierrot and the Factor were already on their way, they would not start in the face of the pitch blackness that would soon shroud the land.

Nepeese shivered and rose to her feet. For the first time Baree got up, and he stood close at her side. Above them a lightning flash cut the clouds like a knife of fire, followed in an instant by a terrific crash of thunder. Baree shrank back as if struck a blow. He would have slunk into the shelter of the brush wall of the wigwam, but there was something about the Willow as he looked at her which gave him confidence. The thunder crashed again. But he retreated no farther. His eyes were fixed on Nepeese.

She stood straight and slim in that gathering gloom riven by the lightning, her beautiful head thrown back, her lips parted, and her eyes glowing with an almost eager anticipation—a sculptured goddess welcoming with bated breath the onrushing forces of the heavens. Perhaps it was because she was born on a night of storm. Many times Pierrot and the dead princess-mother had told her that—how on the night she had come into the world the crash of thunder and the flare of lightning had made the hours an inferno, how the streams had burst over their banks and the stems of

ten thousand forest trees had snapped in its fury—
and the beat of the deluge on their cabin roof had
drowned the sound of her mother's pain, and of her
own first babyish cries.

On that night, it may be, the Spirit of Storm was
born in Nepeese. She loved to face it, as she was facing
it now. It made her forget all things but the splendid
might of nature; her half-wild soul thrilled to the crash
and fire of it; often she had reached up her bare arms
and laughed with joy as the deluge burst about her.
Even now she might have stood there in the little open
until the rain fell, if a whine from Baree had not turned
her. As the first big drops struck with the dull thud of
leaden bullets about them, she went with him into the
balsam shelter.

Once before Baree had passed through a night of
terrible storm—the night he had hidden himself under
a root and saw the tree riven by lightning; but now he
had company, and the warmth and soft pressure of the
Willow's hand on his head and neck filled him with a
strange courage. He growled softly at the crashing
thunder. He wanted to snap at the lightning flashes.
Under her hand Nepeese felt the stiffening of his body,
and in a moment of uncanny stillness she heard the
sharp, uneasy click of his teeth. Then the rain fell.

It was not like other rains Baree had known. It was
an inundation sweeping down out of the blackness of
the skies. Within five minutes the interior of the balsam shelter was a shower-bath—half an hour of that
torrential downpour, and Nepeese was soaked to the
skin. The water ran in little rivulets down her back

and breast; it trickled in tiny streams from her drenched braids and dropped from her long lashes, and the blanket under her was wet as a mop. To Baree it was almost as bad as his near-drowning in the stream after his fight with Papayuchisew, and he snuggled closer and closer under the sheltering arm of the Willow. It seemed an interminable time before the thunder rolled far to the east, and the lightning died away into distant and intermittent flashings. Even after that the rain fell for another hour. Then it stopped as suddenly as it had begun.

With a laughing gasp Nepeese rose to her feet. The water gurgled in her moccasins as she walked out into the open. She paid no attention to Baree—and he followed her. Across the open in the treetops the last of the storm clouds were drifting away. A star shone— then another; and the Willow stood watching them as they appeared until there were so many she could not count. It was no longer black. A wonderful starlight flooded the open after the inky gloom of the storm.

Nepeese looked down and saw Baree. He was standing clear and unleashed, with freedom on all sides of him. Yet he did not run. He was waiting, wet as a water rat, with his eyes on her expectantly. Nepeese made a movement toward him, and hesitated.

"No, you will not run away, Baree. I will leave you free. And now we must have a fire!"

A fire! Anyone but Pierrot might have said that she was crazy. Not a stem or twig in the forest that was not dripping! They could hear the trickle of running water all about them.

"A fire," she said again. "Let us hunt for the *wuskwi*, Baree."

With her wet clothes clinging to her tightly, she was like a slim shadow as she crossed the soggy open and buried herself among the forest trees. Baree still followed. She went straight to a birch tree that she had located that day and began tearing off the loose bark. An armful of this bark she carried close to the wigwam, and on it she heaped load after load of wet wood until she had a great pile. From a bottle in the wigwam she secured a dry match, and at the first touch of its tiny flame the birchbark flared up like paper soaked in oil. Half an hour later the Willow's fire—if there had been no forest walls to hide it—could have been seen at the cabin a mile away. Not until it was blazing a dozen feet into the air did she cease putting wood on it. Then she drove sticks into the soft ground and over these sticks stretched the blanket out to dry. After that she began to undress.

The rain had cooled the air, and the tonic of it— laden with the breath of the balsam and spruce—set the Willow's blood dancing in her veins. She forgot the discomfort of the deluge. She forgot the Factor from Lac Bain, and what Pierrot had told her. After all, she was a bird of the forests, wild with the sweet wildness of the flowers under her bare feet—and in the glory of these wonderful hours that had followed the storm she could see nothing and think of nothing that might harm her. She danced about Baree, tossing her sea of hair about her, her naked body shimmering in and out of it, her eyes aglow, her lips laughing in her unreasoning happiness—the happiness of being alive, of drinking into her lungs the perfumed air of the forest, of seeing the stars and the wonderful sky above her. She stopped before Baree, and cried laughingly at him, holding out her arms:

"*Ahe*, Baree—if you could only throw off your skin as easily as I have thrown off my clothes!

She drew a deep breath, and her eyes shone with a sudden aspiration. Slowly her mouth formed into a round red O, and leaning still nearer to Baree, she whispered:

"It will be deep—and sweet tonight. *Ninga*—yes— we will go!"

She called to him softly as she slipped on her wet moccasins and followed the creek into the forest. A hundred yards from the open she came to the edge of a pool. It was deep and full tonight, three times as big as it had been before the storm. She could hear the gurgle and inrush of water. On its ruffled surface the stars shone. For a moment or two she stood poised on a rock with the cool depths half a dozen feet below her. Then she flung back her hair and shot like a slim white arrow through the starlight.

Baree saw her go. He heard the plunge of her body. For half an hour he lay flat and still, close to the edge of the pool, and watched her. Sometimes she was just under him, floating silently, her hair forming a cloud darker than the water about her; again she was cutting over the surface almost as swiftly as the otters he had seen—and then with a sudden plunge she would disappear, and Baree's heart would quicken its pulse as he waited for her. Once she was gone a long time. He whined. He knew she was not like the beaver and the otter, and he was filled with an immense relief when she came up.

So their first night passed—storm, the cool, deep pool, the big fire; and later, when the Willow's clothes and the blanket had dried, a few hours' sleep. At dawn they returned to the cabin. It was a cautious approach. There was no smoke coming from the chimney. The door was closed. Pierrot and Bush McTaggart were gone.

CHAPTER XVI

IT was the beginning of August—the Flying-up Moon—when Pierrot returned from Lac Bain, and in three days more it would be the Willow's seventeenth birthday. He brought back with him many things for Nepeese—ribbons for her hair, real shoes, which she wore at times like the two Englishwomen at Nelson House, and chief glory of all, some wonderful red cloth for a dress. In the three winters she had spent at the Mission these women had made much of Nepeese. They had taught her to sew as well as to spell and read and pray, and at times there came to the Willow a compelling desire to do as they did.

So for three days Nepeese worked hard on her new dress and on her birthday she stood before Pierrot in a fashion that took his breath away. She had piled her hair in great glowing masses and coils on the crown of her head, as Yvonne, the younger of the English-women, had taught her, and in the rich jet of it had half buried a vivid sprig of the crimson fire-flower. Under this, and the glow in her eyes, and the red flush of her lips and cheeks came the wonderful red dress, fitted to the slim and sinuous beauty of her form—as the style had been two winters ago at Nelson House. And under the dress, which reached just below the knees—Nepeese had quite forgotten the proper length, or else her material had run out—came the *coup de maître* of her toilet, real stockings and the wonderful shoes with high heels! She was a vision before which the gods of the forests might have felt their hearts stop beating. Pierrot turned her round and round without a word, but smiling; but when she left him, followed by Baree, and limping a little in the tightness of her shoes, the smile faded from his face, leaving it cold and staring.

"*Mon Dieu*," he whispered to himself in French, with a thought that was like a sharp stab at his heart, "she is not of her mother's blood—*non*. It is French. She is—yes—like an angel."

There was a change in Pierrot. During the three days of her dressmaking Nepeese had been quite too excited to notice this change, and Pierrot had tried to keep it from her. He had been away ten days on the trip to Lac Bain, and he brought back to Nepeese the

123

joyous news that *M'sieu* McTaggart was very sick with *pechipoo*—the blood poison—news that made the Willow clap her hands and laugh happily. But he knew that the Factor would get well, and that he would come again to their cabin on the Gray Loon. And when next time he came—

It was when he was thinking of this that his face grew cold and hard, and his eyes burned. And he was thinking of it on this her birthday, even as her laughter floated to him like a song. *Dieu*, in spite of her seventeen years, she was nothing but a child—a baby! She could not guess his horrible visions. And the dread of awakening her for all time from that beautiful childhood kept him from telling her the whole truth so that she might have understood fully and completely. *Non*, it should not be that. His soul beat with a great and gentle love. He, Pierrot Du Quesne, would do the watching. And she should laugh and sing and play— and have no share in the black forebodings that had come to spoil his life.

On this day there came up from the south Mac- Donald, the government mapmaker. He was gray and grizzled, with a great, free laugh and a clean heart. Two days he remained with Pierrot. He told Nepeese of his daughters at home, of their mother, whom he worshiped more than anything else on earth—and before he went on in his quest of the last timberline of Banksian pine, he took pictures of the Willow as he had first seen her on her birthday: her hair piled in glossy coils and masses, her red dress, the high-heeled shoes. He carried the negatives on with him, promising Pierrot that he would get a picture back in some way. Thus fate works in its strange and apparently innocent ways as it spins its webs of tragedy.

For many weeks after this there followed tranquil days on the Gray Loon. They were wonderful days for Baree. At first he was suspicious of Pierrot. After a little he tolerated him, and at last accepted him as a part of the cabin—and Nepeese. It was the Willow whose shadow he became. Pierrot noted the attachment with the deepest satisfaction.

"Ah, in a few months more, if he should leap at the throat of *M'sieu* the Factor . . ." he said to himself one day.

In September, when he was six months old, Baree was almost as large as Gray Wolf—big-boned, long-fanged, with a deep chest, and jaws that could already crack a bone as if it were a stick. He was with Nepeese whenever and wherever she moved. They swam together in the two pools—the pool in the forest and the pool between the chasm walls. At first it alarmed Baree to see Nepeese dive from the rock wall over which she had pushed McTaggart, but at the end of a month she had taught him to plunge after her through that twenty feet of space.

It was late in August when Baree saw the first of his kind outside of Kazan and Gray Wolf. During the summer Pierrot allowed his dogs to run at large on a small island in the center of a lake two or three miles away, and twice a week he netted fish for them. On one of these trips Nepeese accompanied him and took

Baree with her. Pierrot carried his long caribou-gut whip. He expected a fight. But there was none. Baree joined the pack in their rush for fish, and ate with them. This pleased Pierrot more than ever.

"He will make a great sledge-dog," he chuckled. "It is best to leave him for a week with the pack, *ma Nepeese.*"

Reluctantly Nepeese gave her consent. While the dogs were still at their fish, they started homeward. Their canoe had stolen well out before Baree discovered the trick they had played on him. Instantly he leaped into the water and swam after them—and the Willow helped him into the canoe.

Early in September a passing Indian brought Pierrot word of Bush McTaggart. The Factor had been very sick. He had almost died from the blood poison, but he was well now. With the first exhilarating tang of autumn in the air a new dread oppressed Pierrot. But at present he said nothing of what was in his mind to Nepeese. The Willow had almost forgotten the Factor from Lac Bain, for the glory and thrill of wilderness autumn was in her blood. She went on long trips with Pierrot, helping him to blaze out the new traplines that would be used when the first snows came, and on these journeys she was always accompanied by Baree.

Most of Nepeese's spare hours she spent in training him for the sledge. She began with a *babiche* string and a stick. It was a whole day before she could induce Baree to drag this stick without turning at every other step to snap and growl at it. Then she fastened another length of *babiche* to him, and made him drag two sticks. Thus little by little she trained him to the sledge harness, until at the end of a fortnight he was tugging heroically at anything she had a mind to fasten him to. Pierrot brought home two of the dogs from the island, and Baree was put into training with these, and helped to drag the empty sledge. Nepeese was delighted. On the day the first light snow fell she clapped her hands and cried to Pierrot:

"By midwinter I will have him the finest dog in the pack, *mon père!*"

This was the time for Pierrot to say what was in his mind. He smiled. *Diantre*—would not that beast the Factor fall into the very devil of a rage when he found how he had been cheated! And yet—

He tried to make his voice quiet and commonplace.

"I am going to send you down to the school at Nelson House again this winter, *ma chérie*," he said. "Baree will help draw you down on the first good snow."

The Willow was tying a knot in Baree's *babiche*, and she rose slowly to her feet and looked at Pierrot. Her eyes were big and dark and steady.

"I am not going, *mon père!*"

It was the first time Nepeese had ever said that to Pierrot—in just that way. It thrilled him. And he could scarcely face the look in her eyes. He was not good at bluffing. She saw what was in his face; it seemed to him that she was reading what was in his mind, and that she grew a little taller as she stood there. Certainly her breath came quicker, and he could see the throb of her breast. Nepeese did not wait for him to gather speech.

"I am not going!" she repeated with even greater finality, and bent again over Baree.

With a shrug of his shoulders Pierrot watched her. After all, was he not glad? Would his heart not have turned sick if she had been happy at the thought of leaving him? He moved to her side and with great gentleness laid a hand on her glossy head. Up from under it the Willow smiled at him. Between them they heard the click of Baree's jaws as he rested his muzzle on the Willow's arm. For the first time in weeks the world seemed suddenly filled with sunshine for Pierrot. When he went back to the cabin he held his head higher. Nepeese would not leave him! He laughed softly. He rubbed his hands together. His fear of the Factor from Lac Bain was gone. From the cabin door he looked back at Nepeese and Baree.

"The Saints be blessed!" he murmured. "Now— now—it is Pierrot Du Quesne who knows what to do!"

CHAPTER XVII

BACK to Lac Bain, late in September, came MacDonald the mapmaker. For ten days Gregson, the Investigating Agent, had been Bush McTaggart's guest at the Post, and twice in that time it had come into Marie's mind to creep upon him while he slept and kill him. The Factor himself paid little attention to her now, a fact which would have made her happy if it had not been for Gregson. He was enraptured with the wild, sinuous beauty of the Cree girl, and McTaggart, without jealousy, encouraged him. He was tired of Marie.

McTaggart told Gregson this. He wanted to get rid of her, and if he—Gregson—could possibly take her on with him it would be a great favor. He explained why. A little later, when the deep snows came, he was going to bring the daughter of Pierrot Du Quesne to the Post. In the rottenness of their brotherhood he told of his visit, of the manner of his reception, and of the incident at the chasm. In spite of all this, he assured Gregson. Pierrot's girl would soon be at Lac Bain.

It was at this time that MacDonald came. He remained only one night, and without knowing that he was adding fuel to a fire already dangerously blazing, he gave the photograph he had taken of Nepeese to the Factor. It was a splendid picture.

"If you can get it down to that girl someday I'll be mightily obliged," he said to McTaggart. "I promised her one. Her father's name is Du Quesne—Pierrot Du Quesne. You probably know them. And the girl—"

His blood warmed as he described to McTaggart how beautiful she was that day in her red dress, which had taken black in the photograph. He did not guess how near the boiling piont McTaggart's blood was.

The next day MacDonald started for Norway House. McTaggart did not show Gregson the picture. He kept it to himself, and at night, under the glow of his lamp, he looked at it with thoughts that filled him with a growing resolution. There was but one way. The scheme had been in his mind for weeks—and the picture determined him. He dared not whisper his secret even to Gregson. But it was the one way. It would give him Nepeese. Only—he must wait for the deep snows, the midwinter snows. They buried their tragedies deepest.

McTaggart was glad when Gregson followed the mapmaker to Norway House. Out of courtesy he accompanied him a day's journey on his way. When he returned to the Post, Marie was gone. He was glad. He sent off a runner with a load of presents for her people, and the message: "Don't beat her. Keep her. She is free."

Along with the bustle and stir of the beginning of the trapping season McTaggart began to prepare his house for the coming of Nepeese. He knew what she liked in the way of cleanliness and a few other things. He had the log walls painted white with the lead and oil that were intended for his York boats. Certain partitions were torn down, and new ones were built; the Indian wife of his chief runner made curtains for the windows, and he confiscated a small phonograph that should have gone on to Lac la Biche. He had no doubts, and he counted the days as they passed.

Down on the Gray Loon, Pierrot and Nepeese were busy at many things, so busy that at times Pierrot's fears of the Factor at Lac Bain were forgotten, and they went out of the Willow's mind entirely. It was the Red Moon, and it thrilled with the anticipation and excitement of the winter hunt. Nepeese carefully dipped a hundred traps in boiling caribou fat mixed with beaver grease, while Pierrot made fresh deadfalls ready for setting on his trails. When he was gone more than a day from the cabin, she was always with him.

But at the cabin there was much to do, for Pierrot, like all his Northern brotherhood, did not begin to prepare until the keen tang of autumn was in the air. There were snowshoes to be rewebbed with new *babiche*, there was wood to be cut in readiness for the winter storms; the cabin had to be banked, a new harness made, skinning knives sharpened and winter moccasins to be manufactured—a hundred and one affairs to be attended to, even to the repairing of the meat rack at the back of the cabin, where, from the beginning of cold weather until the end, would hang the haunches of deer, caribou, and moose for the family larder and, when fish were scarce, the dogs' rations.

In the bustle of all this Nepeese was compelled to give less attention to Baree than during the preceding weeks. They did not play so much; they no longer swam, for with the mornings there was deep frost on the ground, and the water was turning icy cold: they no longer wandered deep in the forest after flowers and berries. For hours at a time Baree would now lie at the Willow's feet, watching her slender fingers as they weaved swiftly in and out with her snowshoe *babiche*; and now and then Nepeese would pause to lean over and put her hand on his head, and talk to him for a moment—sometimes in her soft Cree, sometimes in English or her father's French.

It was the Willow's voice which Baree had learned

to understand, and the movement of her lips, her gesture, the poise of her body, the changing moods which brought shadow or sunlight into her face. He knew what it meant when she smiled; he shook himself, and often jumped about her in sympathetic rejoicing, when she laughed; her happiness was a part of him, a stern word from her was worse than a blow. Twice Pierrot had struck him, and twice Baree had sprang back and faced him with bared fangs and an angry snarl, the crest along his back standing up like a brush. Had one of the other dogs done this, Pierrot would have half killed him. It would have been mutiny, and the man must be master. But Baree was always safe. A touch of the Willow's hand, a word from her lips, and the crest slowly settled and the snarl went out of his throat.

Pierrot was not at all displeased.

"*Dieu*. I will never go so far as to try and whip that out of him," he told himself. "He is a barbarian—a wild beast—and her slave. For her he would kill!"

So it came, through Pierrot himself—and without telling his reason for it—that Baree did not become a sledge-dog. He was allowed his freedom, and was never tied, like the others. Nepeese was glad, but did not guess the thought that was in Pierrot's mind. To himself Pierrot chuckled. She would never know why he kept Baree always suspicious of him, even to the point of hating him. It required considerable skill and cunning on his part. With himself he reasoned:

"If I make him hate me, he will hate all men. *Meyoo!* That is good."

So he looked into the future—for Nepeese.

Now the tonic-filled days and cold, frosty nights of the Red Moon brought about the big change in Baree. It was inevitable. Pierrot knew that it would come, and the first night that Baree settled back on his haunches and howled up at the Red Moon, Pierrot prepared Nepeese for it.

"He is a wild dog, *ma Nepeese*," he said to her. "He is half wolf, and the Call will come to him strong. He will go into the forests. He will disappear at times. But we must not fasten him. He will come back. *Ka*, he will come back!" And he rubbed his hands in the moonglow until his knuckles cracked.

The Call came to Baree like a thief entering slowly and cautiously into a forbidden place. He did not understand it at first. It made him nervous and uneasy, so restless that Nepeese frequently heard him whine softly in his sleep. He was waiting for something. What was it? Pierrot knew, and smiled in his inscrutable way.

And then it came. It was night, a glorious night filled with moon and stars, under which the earth was whitening with a film of frost, when they heard the first hunt call of the wolves. Now and then during the summer there had come the lone wolf howl, but this was the tonguing of the pack; and as it floated through the vast silence and mystery of the night, a song of savagery that had come with each Red Moon down through unending ages, Pierrot knew that at last had come that for which Baree had been waiting.

In an instant Baree had sensed it. His muscles grew taut as pieces of stretched rope as he stood up in the moonlight, facing the direction from which floated the mystery and thrill of the sound. They could hear him whining softly; and Pierrot, bending down so that he caught the light of the night properly, could see him trembling.

"It is *Mee-Koo!*" he said in a whisper to Nepeese.

That was it, the call of the blood that was running swift in Baree's veins—not alone the call of his species, but the call of Kazan and Gray Wolf and of his forebears for generations unnumbered. It was the voice of his people. So Pierrot had whispered, and he was right. In the golden night the Willow was waiting, for it was she who had gambled most, and it was she who must lose or win. She uttered no sound, replied not to the low voice of Pierrot, but held her breath and watched Baree as he slowly faded away, step by step, in the shadows. In a few moments more he was gone. It was then that she stood straight, and flung back her head, with eyes that glowed in rivalry with the stars.

"Baree!" she called. "Baree! Baree! Baree!"

He must have been near the edge of the forest, for she had drawn a slow, waiting breath or two before he was back at her side. But he had come, straight as an arrow, and he whined up into her face. Nepeese put her hands to his head.

"You are right, *mon père*," she said. "He will go to the wolves, but he will come back. He will never leave me for long." With one hand still on Baree's head, she pointed with the other into the pitlike blackness of the forest. "Go to them, Baree!" she whispered. "But you must come back. You must. *Cheamao!*"

With Pierrot she went into the cabin; the door closed behind them, and Baree was alone. There was a long silence. In it he could hear the soft night sounds: the clinking of the chains to which the dogs were fastened, the restless movement of their bodies, the throbbing whir of a pair of wings, the breath of the night itself. For to him this night, even in its stillness, seemed alive. Again he went into it, and close to the forest once more he stopped to listen. The wind had turned, and on it rode the wailing, blood-thrilling cry of the pack. Far off to the west a lone wolf turned his muzzle to the sky and answered that gathering call of his clan; and then out of the east came a voice, so far beyond the cabin that it was like an echo dying away in the vastness of the night.

A choking note gathered in Baree's throat. He threw up his head. Straight above him was the Red Moon, inviting him to the thrill and mystery of the open world. The sound grew in his throat, and slowly it rose in volume until his answer was rising to the stars. In their cabin Pierrot and the Willow heard it. Pierrot shrugged his shoulders.

"He is gone," he said.

"*Oui*, he is gone, *mon père*," replied Nepeese, peering through the window.

CHAPTER XVIII

NO longer, as in the days of old, did the darkness of the forests hold a fear for Baree. This night his hunt cry had risen to the stars and the moon, and in that cry he had, for the first time, sent forth his defiance of night and space, his warning to all the wild, and his acceptance of the Brotherhood. In that cry, and the answers that came back to him, he sensed a new power—the final triumph of nature in impinging on him the fact that the forests and the creatures they held were no longer to be feared, but that all things feared him. Off there, beyond the pale of the cabin and the influence of Nepeese, were all the things that the wolf-blood in him found now most desirable: companionship of his kind, the lure of adventure, the red, sweet blood of the chase—and matehood. This last, after all, was the dominant mystery that was urging him, and yet least of all did he understand it.

He ran straight into the darkness to the north and west, slinking low under the bushes, his tail drooping, his ears aslant—the wolf as the wolf runs on the night trail. The pack had swung due north, and was traveling faster than he, so that at the end of half an hour he could no longer hear it. But the lone wolf howl to the west was nearer, and three times Baree gave answer to it.

At the end of an hour he heard the pack again, swinging southward. Pierrot would easily have understood. Their quarry had found safety beyond water, or in a lake, and the *muhekuns* were on a fresh trail. By this time not more than a quarter of a mile of the forest separated Baree from the lone wolf, but the lone wolf was also an old wolf, and with the directness and precision of long experience, he swerved in the direction of the hunters, compassing his trail so that he was heading for a point half or three-quarters of a mile in advance of the pack.

This was a trick of the Brotherhood which Baree had yet to learn; and the result of his ignorance, and lack of skill, was that twice within the next half-hour he found himself near to the pack without being able to join it. Then came a long and final silence. The pack had pulled down its kill, and in their feasting they made no sound.

The rest of the night Baree wandered alone, or at least until the moon was well on the wane. He was a long way from the cabin, and his trail had been an uncertain and twisting one, but he was no longer possessed with the discomforting sensation of being lost. The last two or three months had been developing strongly in him the sense of orientation, that "sixth sense" which guides the pigeon unerringly on its way and takes a bear straight as a bird might fly to its last year's denning-place.

Baree had not forgotten Nepeese. A dozen times he turned his head back and whined, and always he picked out accurately the direction in which the cabin lay. But he did not turn back. As the night lengthened, his search for that mysterious something which he had not found continued. His hunger, even with the fading

137

out of the moon and the coming of the gray dawn, was not sufficiently keen to make him hunt for food.

It was cold, and it seemed colder when the glow of the moon and stars died out. Under his padded feet, especially in the open spaces, was a thick white frost in which he left clearly at times the imprint of his toes and claws. He had traveled steadily for hours, a great many miles in all, and he was tired when the first light of the day came. And then there came the time when, with a sudden sharp click of his jaws, he stopped like a shot in his tracks.

At last it had come—the meeting with that for which he had been seeking. It was in an open, lighted by the cold dawn—a tiny amphitheater that lay on the side of a ridge, facing the east. With her head toward him, and waiting for him as he came out of the shadows, his scent strong in her keen nose, stood Maheegun, the young wolf. Baree had not smelled her, but he saw her directly he came out of the rim of young balsams that fringed the open. It was then he stopped, and for a full minute neither of them moved a muscle or seemed to breathe.

There was not a fortnight's difference in their age and yet Maheegun was much the smaller of the two; her body was as long, but she was slimmer; she stood on slender legs that were almost like the legs of a fox, and the curve of her back was that of a slightly bent bow, a sign of swiftness almost equal to the wind. She stood poised for flight even as Baree advanced his first step toward her, and then very slowly her body relaxed, and in a direct ratio as he drew nearer her ears lost their alertness and dropped aslant.

Baree whined. His own ears were up, his head alert, his tail aloft and bushy. Cleverness, if not strategy, had already become a part of his masculine superiority, and he did not immediately press the affair. He was within five feet of Maheegun when he casually turned away from her and faced the east, where a faint penciling of red and gold was heralding the day. For a few moments he sniffed and looked around and pointed the wind with much seriousness, as though impressing on his fair acquaintance—as many a two-legged animal has done before him—his tremendous importance in the world at large.

And Maheegun was properly impressed. Baree's bluff worked as beautifully as the bluffs of the two-legged animals. He sniffed the air with such thrilling and suspicious zeal that Maheegun's ears sprang alert, and she sniffed it with him; he turned his head from point to point so sharply and alertly that her feminine curiosity, if not anxiety, made her turn her own head in questioning conjunction; and when he whined, as though in the air he had caught a mystery which she could not possibly understand, a responsive note gathered in her throat, but smothered and low as a woman's exclamation when she is not quite sure whether she should interrupt her lord or not. At this sound, which Baree's sharp ears caught, he swung up to her with a light and mincing step, and in another moment they were smelling noses.

When the sun rose, half an hour later, it found them still in the small open on the side of the ridge, with a deep fringe of forest under them, and beyond that a wide, timbered plain which looked like a ghostly shroud in its mantle of frost. Up over this came the first red glow of the day, filling the open with a warmth that grew more and more comfortable as the sun crept higher.

Neither Baree nor Maheegun was inclined to move for a while, and for an hour or two they lay basking in a cup of the slope, looking down with questing and wide-awake eyes upon the wooded plain that stretched away under them like a great sea.

Maheegun, too, had sought the hunt pack, and like Baree had failed to catch it. They were tired, a little discouraged for the time, and hungry—but still alive with the fine thrill of anticipation, and restlessly sensitive to the new and mysterious consciousness of companionship. Half a dozen times Baree got up and nosed about Maheegun as she lay in the sun, whining to her softly and touching her soft coat with his muzzle, but for a long time she paid little attention to him. At last she followed him. All that day they wandered and rested together. Once more the night came.

It was without moon or stars. Gray masses of clouds swept slowly down out of the north and east, and in the treetops there was scarcely a whisper of wind as night gathered in. The snow began to fall at dusk, thickly, heavily, without a breath of sound. It was not cold, but it was still—so still that Baree and Maheegun traveled only a few yards at a time, and then stopped to listen. In this way all the night-prowlers of the forest were traveling, if they were moving at all. It was the first of the Big Snow.

To the flesh-eating wild things of the forests, clawed and winged, the Big Snow was the beginning of the winter carnival of slaughter and feasting, of wild adventure in the long nights, of merciless warfare on the frozen trails. The days of breeding, of motherhood—the peace of spring and summer—were over; out of the sky came the wakening of the Northland, the call of all flesh-eating creatures to the long hunt, and in the first thrill of it, living things were moving but little this night, and that watchfully and with suspicion. Youth made it all new to Baree and Maheegun; their blood ran swiftly; their feet fell softly; their ears were attuned to catch the slightest sounds.

In this first of the Big Snow they felt the exciting pulse of a new life. It lured them on. It invited them to adventure into the white mystery of the silent storm; and inspired by that restlessness of youth and its desires, they went on.

The snow grew deeper under their feet. In the open spaces they waded through it to their knees, and it continued to fall in a vast white cloud that descended steadily out of the sky. It was near midnight when it stopped. The clouds drifted away from under the stars and the moon, and for a long time Baree and Maheegun stood without moving, looking down from the bald crest of a ridge upon a wonderful world.

Never had they seen so far, except in the light of day. Under them was a plain. They could see its forests, lone trees that stood up like shadows out of the snow, a stream—still unfrozen—shimmering like glass with the flicker of forelight on it. Toward this stream Baree led the way. He no longer thought of Nepeese, and he whined with pent-up happiness as he stopped halfway down and turned to muzzle Maheegun. He wanted to roll in the snow and frisk about with his companion; he wanted to bark, to put up his head and howl as he had howled at the Red Moon back at the cabin.

Something held him from doing these things. Perhaps it was Maheegun's demeanor. She accepted his attentions rigidly. Once or twice she had seemed almost frightened; twice Baree had heard the sharp clicking of her teeth. The previous night, and all through tonight's storm, their companionship had grown more intimate, but now there was taking its place a mysterious aloofness on the part of Maheegun. Pierrot could have explained. With the white snow under and about him, and the luminous moon and stars above him, Baree, like the night, had undergone a transformation which even the sunlight of day had not made in him before. His coat was like polished jet. Every hair in his body glistened black. *Black!* That was it. And Nature was trying to tell Maheegun that of all the creatures hated by her kind, the creature which they feared and hated most was black. With her it was not experience, but instinct—telling her of the age-old feud between the gray wolf and the black bear. And Baree's coat, in the moonlight and the snow, was blacker then Wakayoo's had ever been in the fish-fattening days of May. Until they struck the broad openings of the plain, the young she-wolf had followed Baree without hesitation; now there was a gathering strangeness and indecision in her manner, and twice she stopped and would have let Baree go on without her.

An hour after they entered the plain there came suddenly out of the west the tonguing of the wolf pack. It was not far distant, probably not more than a mile along the foot of the ridge, and the sharp, quick yapping that followed the first outburst was evidence that the long-fanged hunters had put up sudden game, a caribou or young moose, and were close at its heels. At the voice of her own people Maheegun laid her ears close to her head and was off like an arrow from a bow.

The unexpectedness of her movement and the swiftness of her flight put Baree well behind her in the race over the plain. She was running blindly, favored by luck. For an interval of perhaps five minutes the pack were so near to their game that they made no sound, and the chase swung full into the face of Maheegun and Baree. The latter was not half a dozen lengths behind the young wolf when a crashing in the brush directly ahead stopped them so sharply that they tore up the snow with their braced forefeet and squat haunches. Ten seconds later a caribou burst through and flashed across an open not more than twenty yards from where they stood. They could hear its swift panting as it disappeared. And then came the pack.

At sight of those swiftly moving gray bodies Baree's heart leaped for an instant into his throat. He forgot Maheegun, and that she had run away from him. The moon and the stars went out of existence for him. He no longer sensed the chill of the snow under his feet. He was wolf—all wolf. With the warm scent of the caribou in his nostrils, and the passion to kill sweeping through him like fire, he darted after the pack.

Even at that, Maheegun was a bit ahead of him. He did not miss her; in the excitement of his first chase he no longer felt the desire to have her at his side. Very soon he found himself close to the flanks of one of the gray monsters of the pack; half a minute later a new hunter swept in from the bush behind him, and then a second, and after that a third. At times he was running shoulder to shoulder with his new companions; he heard the whining excitement in their throats; the snap of their jaws as they ran—and in the golden moonlight ahead of him the smash of the caribou as it plunged through thickets and over windfalls in its race for life.

It was as if Baree had belonged to the pack always. He had joined it naturally, as other stray wolves had joined it from out of the bush; there had been no ostentation, no welcome such as Meheegun had given him in the open, and no hostility. He belonged with these slim, swift-footed outlaws of the old forests, and his own jaws snapped and his blood ran hot as the smell of the caribou grew heavier, and the sound of its crashing body nearer.

It seemed to him they were almost at its heel when they swept into an open plain, a stretch of barren without a tree or a shrub, brilliant in the light of the stars and moon. Across its unbroken carpet of snow sped the caribou a spare hundred years ahead of the pack. Now the two leading hunters no longer followed directly in the trail, but shot out at an angle, one to the right and the other to the left of the pursued, and like well-trained soldiers the pack split in halves and spread out fanshape in the final charge.

The two ends of the fan forged ahead and closed in, until the leaders were running almost abreast of the caribou, with fifty or sixty feet separating them from the pursued. Thus, adroitly and swiftly, with deadly precision, the pack had formed a horseshoe cordon of fangs from which there was but one course of flight— straight ahead. For the caribou to swerve half a degree to the right or left meant death. It was the duty of the leaders to draw in the ends of the horseshoe now, until one or both of them could make the fatal lunge for the hamstrings. After that it would be a simple matter. The pack would close in over the caribou like an inundation.

Baree had found his place in the lower rim of the horseshoe, so that he was fairly well in the rear when the climax came. The plain made a sudden dip. Straight ahead was the gleam of water—water shimmering softly in the starglow, and the sight of it sent a final great spurt of blood through the caribou's bursting heart. Forty seconds would tell the story—forty seconds of a last spurt for life, of a final tremendous effort to escape death. Baree felt the sudden thrill of these moments, and he forged ahead with the others in the lower rim of the horseshoe as one of the leading wolves made a lunge for the young bull's hamstrings. It was a clean miss. A second wolf darted in. And this one also missed.

There was no time for others to take their place.

From the broken end of the horseshoe Baree heard the caribou's heavy plunge into water. When Baree joined the pack, a maddened, mouth-frothing, snarling horde, Napamoos, the young bull, was well out in the river and swimming steadily for the opposite shore.

It was then that Baree found himself at the side of Maheegun. She was panting; her red tongue hung from her open jaws; but at his presence she brought her fangs together with a snap and slunk from him into the heart of the wind-run and disappointed pack. The wolves were in an ugly temper, but Baree did not sense the fact. Nepeese had trained him to take to water like an otter, and he did not understand why this narrow river should stop them as it had. He ran down to the water and stood belly deep in it, facing for an instant the horde of savage beasts above him, wondering why they did not follow. And he was black—*black*. He came among them again, and for the first time they noticed him.

The restless movements of the waters ceased now. A new and wondering interest held them rigid. Fangs closed sharply. A little in the open Baree saw Maheegun, with a big gray wolf standing near her. He went to her again, and this time she remained with flattened ears until he was sniffing her neck. And then, with a vicious snarl, she snapped at him. Her teeth sank deep in the soft flesh of his shoulder, and at the unexpectedness and pain of her attack, he let out a yelp. The next instant the big gray wolf was at him.

Again caught unexpectedly, Baree went down with the wolf's fangs at his throat. But in him was the blood of Kazan, the flesh and bone and sinew of Kazan, and for the first time in his life he fought as Kazan fought on that terrible day at the top of the Sun Rock. He was young; he had yet to learn the cleverness and the strategy of the veteran; but his jaws were like the iron clamps with which Pierrot set his bear traps, and in his heart was sudden and blinding rage, a desire to kill that rose above all sense of pain or fear.

That fight, if it had been fair, would have been a victory for Baree, even in his youth and inexperience. In fairness the pack should have waited; it was a law of the pack to wait—until one was done for. But Baree was black; he was a stranger, an interloper, a creature whom they noticed now in a moment when their blood was hot with the rage and disappointment of killers who had missed their prey. A second wolf sprang in, striking Baree treacherously from the flank; and while he was in the snow, his jaws crushing the foreleg of his first foe, the pack was on him *en masse*.

Such an attack on the young caribou bull would have meant death in less than a minute. Every fang would have found its hold. Baree, by the fortunate circumstance that he was under his first two assailants and protected by their bodies, was saved from being torn instantly into pieces. He knew that he was fighting for his life. Over him the horde of beasts rolled and twisted and snarled; he felt the burning pain of teeth sinking into his flesh; he was smothered; a hundred knives seemed cutting him into pieces; yet no sound—not a whimper or a cry—came from him now in the horror and hopelessness of it all.

It would have ended in another half-minute had the struggle not been at the very edge of the bank. Undermined by the erosion of the spring floods, a section of this bank suddenly gave way, and with it went Baree and half the pack. In a flash Baree thought of the water and the escaping caribou. For a bare instant the cave-in had sent him free of the pack, and in that space he gave a single leap over the gray backs of his enemies into the deep water of the stream. Close behind him half a dozen jaws snapped shut on empty air. As it had saved the caribou, so this strip of water shimmering in the glow of the moon and stars had saved Baree.

The stream was not more than a hundred feet in width, but it cost Baree close to a losing struggle to get across it. Until he dragged himself out on the opposite shore, the extent of his injuries was not impressed upon him fully. One hind leg, for the time, was useless; his forward left shoulder was laid open to the bone; his head and body were torn and cut; and as he dragged himself slowly away from the stream, the trail he left in the snow was a red path of blood. It trickled from his panting jaws, between which his tongue was bleeding; it ran down his legs and flanks and belly, and it dripped from his ears, one of which was slit clean for two inches as though cut with a knife. His instincts were dazed, his perception of things clouded as if by a veil drawn close over his eyes. He did not hear, a few minutes later, the howling of the disappointed wolf horde on the other side of the river, and he no longer sensed the existence of moon or stars. Half dead, he dragged himself on until by chance he came to a clump of dwarf spruce. Into this he struggled, and then he dropped exhausted.

All that night and until noon the next day Baree lay without moving. The fever burned in his blood; it flamed high and swift toward death; then it ebbed slowly, and life conquered. At noon he came forth. He was weak, and he wobbled on his legs. His hind leg still dragged, and he was racked with pain. But it was a splendid day. The sun was warm; the snow was thawing; the sky was like a great blue sea; and the floods of life coursed warmly again through Baree's veins. But now, for all time, his desires were changed, and his great quest at an end.

A red ferocity grew in Baree's eyes as he snarled in the direction of last night's fight with the wolves. They were no longer his people. They were no longer of his blood. Never again could the hunt call lure him or the voice of the pack rouse the old longing. In him there was a thing newborn, an undying hatred for the wolf, a hatred that was to grow in him until it became like a disease in his vitals, a thing ever present and insistent, demanding vengeance on their kind. Last night he had gone to them a comrade. Today he was an outcast. Cut and maimed, bearing with him scars for all time, he had learned his lesson of the wilderness. Tomorrow, and the next day, and for days after that without number, he would remember the lesson well.

CHAPTER XIX

AT the cabin on the Gray Loon, on the fourth night of Baree's absence, Pierrot was smoking his pipe after a great supper of caribou tenderloin he had brought in from the trail, and Nepeese was listening to his tale of the remarkable shot he had made, when a sound at the door interrupted them. Nepeese opened it, and Baree came in. The cry of welcome that was on the girl's lips died there instantly, and Pierrot stared as if he could not quite believe this creature that had returned was the wolf-dog. Three days and nights of hunger in which he could not hunt because of the leg that dragged had put on him the marks of starvation. Battle-scarred and covered with dried blood clots that still clung tenaciously to his long hair, he was a sight that drew at last a long breath from Nepeese. A queer smile was growing in Pierrot's face as he leaned forward in his chair; and then slowly rising to his feet, and looking closer, he said to Nepeese:

"*Ventre Saint Gris! Oui*, he has been to the pack, Nepeese, and the pack turned on him. It was not a two-wolf fight—*non*! It was the pack. He is cut and torn in fifty places. And—*mon Dieu*, he is alive!"

In Pierrot's voice there was growing wonder and amazement. He was incredulous, and yet he could not disbelieve what his eyes told him. What had happened was nothing short of a miracle, and for a time he uttered not a word more but remained staring in silence while Nepeese woke from her astonishment to give Baree doctoring and food. After he had eaten ravenously of cold boiled mush she began bathing his wounds in warm water, and after that she soothed them with bear grease, talking to him all the time in her soft Cree. After the pain and hunger and treachery of his adventure, it was a wonderful homecoming for Baree. He slept that night at the foot of the Willow's bed. The next morning it was the cool caress of his tongue on her hand that awakened her.

With this day they resumed the comradeship interrupted by Baree's temporary desertion. The attachment was greater than ever on Baree's part. It was he who had run away from the Willow, who had deserted her at the call of the pack, and it seemed at times as though he sensed the depths of his perfidy and was striving to make amends. There was indubitably a very great change in him. He hung to Nepeese like a shadow. Instead of sleeping at night in the spruce shelter Pierrot made for him, he made himself a little hollow in the earth close to the cabin door. Pierrot thought that he understood, and Nepeese thought that she understood still more; but in reality the key to the mystery remained with Baree himself. He no longer played as he had played before he went off alone into the forest. He did not chase sticks, or run until he was winded, for the pure joy of running. His puppyishness was gone. In its place was a great worship and a rankling bitterness, a love for the girl and a hatred for the pack and all that it stood for. Whenever he heard the wolf howl, it brought an angry snarl into his throat, and he would bare his fangs until even Pierrot would draw a little away from him. But a touch of the girl's hand would quiet him.

In a week or two the heavier snows came, and Pierrot began making his trips over the traplines. Nepeese had entered into a thrilling bargain with him this winter. Pierrot had taken her into partnership. Every fifth trap, every fifth deadfall, and every fifth poison bait was to be her own, and what they caught or killed was to bring a bit nearer to realization a wonderful dream that was growing in the Willow's soul. Pierrot had promised. If they had great luck that winter, they would go down together on the last snows to Nelson House and buy the little old organ that was for sale there; and if the organ was sold, they would work another winter, and get a new one.

This plan gave Nepeese an enthusiastic and tireless interest in the trapline. With Pierrot it was more or less a fine bit of strategy. He would have sold his hand to give Nepeese the organ; he was determined that she should have it, whether the fifth traps and the fifth deadfalls and the fifth poison baits caught the fur or not. The partnership meant nothing so far as that was concerned. But in another way it meant to Nepeese a business interest, the thrill of personal achievement. Pierrot impressed on her that it made a comrade and co-worker of her on the trail. That was his scheme: to keep her with him when he was away from the cabin. He knew that Bush McTaggart would come again to the Gray Loon, probably more than once during the winter. He had swift dogs, and it was a short journey.

And when McTaggart came, Nepeese must not be at the cabin—alone.

Pierrot's trapline swung into the north and west, covering in all a matter of fifty miles, with an average of two traps, one deadfall, and a poison bait to each mile. It was a twisting line blazed along streams for mink, otter, and marten, piercing the deepest forests for fisher cat and lynx and crossing lakes and storm-swept strips of barrens where poison baits could be set for fox and wolf. Halfway over this line Pierrot had built a small log cabin, and at the end of it another, so that a day's work meant twenty-five miles. This was easy for Pierrot, and not hard on Nepeese after the first few days.

All through October and November they made the trips regularly, making the round every six days, which gave one day of rest at the cabin on the Gray Loon and another day in the cabin at the end of the trail. To Pierrot the winter's work was business, the labor of his people for many generations back; to Nepeese and Baree it was a wild and joyous adventure that never for a day grew tiresome. Even Pierrot could not quite immunize himself against their enthusiasm. It was infectious, and he was happier than he had been since his sun had set that evening the princess-mother died.

They were splendid months. Fur was thick, and it was steadily cold without bad storms. Nepeese not only carried a small pack on her shoulders in order that Pierrot's load might be lighter, but she trained Baree to bear tiny shoulder panniers which she manufac-

153

tured. In these panniers Baree carried the bait. In at least a third of the total number of traps set there was always what Pierrot called trash—rabbits, owls, whisky-jacks, jays, and squirrels. These, with the skin or feathers stripped off, made up the bulk of the bait for the traps ahead.

One afternoon early in December, as they were returning to the Gray Loon, Pierrot stopped suddenly a dozen paces ahead of Nepeese and stared at the snow. A strange snowshoe trail had joined their own and was heading toward the cabin. For half a minute Pierrot was silent and scarcely moved a muscle as he stared. The trail came straight out of the north—and off there was Lac Bain. Also they were the marks of large snowshoes, and the stride indicated was that of a tall man. Before Pierrot had spoken, Nepeese had guessed what they meant.

"*M'sieu* the Factor from Lac Bain!" she said.

Baree was sniffing suspiciously at the strange trail. They heard the low growl in his throat, and Pierrot's shoulders stiffened.

"Yes, the *M'sieu*," he said.

The Willow's heart beat more swiftly as they went on. She was not afraid of McTaggart, not physically afraid; and yet something rose up in her breast and choked her at thought of his presence on the Gray Loon. Why was he there? It was not necessary for Pierrot to answer the question, even had she given voice to it. She knew. The Factor from Lac Bain had no business there—except to see her. The blood burned red in her cheeks as she thought again of that minute on the edge of the chasm when he had almost crushed her in his arms. Would he try *that* again?

Pierrot, deep in his own sombre thoughts, scarcely heard the strange laugh that came suddenly from her lips. Nepeese was listening to the growl that was again in Baree's throat. It was a low but terrible sound. When half a mile from the cabin, she unslung the panniers from his shoulders and carried them herself. Ten minutes later they saw a man advancing to meet them.

It was not McTaggart. Pierrot recognized him, and with an audible breath of relief waved his hand. It was DeBar, who trapped in the Barren Country north of Lac Bain. Pierrot knew him well. They had exchanged fox poison. They were friends, and there was pleasure in the grip of their hands. DeBar stared then at Nepeese.

"*Tonnerre*, she has grown into a woman!" he cried, and like a woman Nepeese looked at him straight, with the color deepening in her cheeks, as he bowed low with a courtesy that dated back a couple of centuries beyond the trapline.

DeBar lost no time in explaining his mission, and before they reached the cabin Pierrot and Nepeese knew why he had come. *M'sieu* the Factor at Lac Bain was leaving on a journey in five days, and he had sent DeBar as a special messenger to request Pierrot to come up to assist the clerk and the halfbreed storekeeper in his absence. Pierrot made no comment at first. But he was thinking. Why had Bush McTaggart sent for *him*? Why had he not chosen someone nearer? Not until a fire was crackling in the sheet-iron stove

155

in the cabin, and Nepeese was busily engaged getting supper, did he voice these questions to the fox hunter.

DeBar shrugged his shoulders.

"He asked me, at first, if I could stay. But I have a wife with a bad lung, Pierrot. It was caught by frost last winter, and I dare not leave her long alone. He has great faith in you. Besides, you know all the trappers on the company's books at Lac Bain. So he sent for you, and begs you not to worry about your fur lines, as he will pay you double what you would catch in the time you are at the Post."

"And—Nepeese?" said Pierrot. "*M'sieu* expects me to bring her?"

From the stove the Willow bent her head to listen, and her heart leaped free again at DeBar's answer.

"He said nothing about that. But surely—it will be a great change for li'le *m'selle.*"

Pierrot nodded.

"Possibly, *Netootam.*"

They discussed the matter no more that night. But for hours Pierrot was still, thinking, and a hundred times he asked himself that same question: Why had McTaggart sent for *him*? He was not the only man well known to the trappers on the company's books. There was Wassoon, for instance, the halfbreed Scandinavian whose cabin was less than four hours' journey from the post—or Baroche, the white-bearded old Frenchman who lived yet nearer and whose word was as good as the Bible. It must be, he told himself finally, that *M'sieu* had sent for *him* because he wanted to win over the father of Nepeese and gain the friendship of Nepeese herself. For this was undoubtedly a very great honor that the Factor was conferring on him. And yet, deep down in his heart, he was filled with suspicion.

When DeBar was about to leave the next morning, Pierrot said: "Tell *M'sieu* that I will leave for Lac Bain the day after tomorrow.

After DeBar had gone, he said to Nepeese:

"And you shall remain here, *ma chérie*. I will not take you to Lac Bain. I have had a dream that *M'sieu* will not go on a journey, but that he has lied, and that he will be *sick* when I arrive at the post. And yet, if it should happen that you care to go—"

Nepeese straightened suddenly, like a reed that has been caught by the wind.

"*Non!*" she cried, so fiercely that Pierrot laughed, and rubbed his hands.

So it happened that on the second day after the fox hunter's visit Pierrot left for Lac Bain, with Nepeese in the door waving him good-bye until he was out of sight.

On the morning of this same day Bush McTaggart rose from his bed while it was still dark. The time had come. He had hesitated at murder—at the killing of Pierrot; and in his hesitation he had found a better way. There could be no escape for Nepeese.

It was a wonderful scheme, so easy of accomplishment, so inevitable in its outcome. And all the time Pierrot would think he was away to the east on a mission!

He ate his breakfast before dawn, and was on the trail before it was yet light. Purposely he struck due east, so that in coming up from the south and west Pierrot would not strike his sledge tracks. For he had made up his mind now that Pierrot must never know and must never have a suspicion, even though it cost him so many more miles to travel that he would not reach the Gray Loon until the second day. It was better to be a day late, after all, as it was possible that something might have delayed Pierrot. So he made no effort to travel fast.

There was a vast amount of brutal satisfaction to McTaggart in anticipating what was about to happen, and he reveled in it to the full. There was no chance for disappointment. He was positive that Nepeese would not accompany her father to Lac Bain. She would be at the cabin on the Gray Loon—alone.

This aloneness was to Nepeese burdened with no thought of danger. There were times, now, when the thought of being alone was pleasant to her, when she wanted to dream by herself, when she visioned things into the mysteries of which she would not admit even Pierrot. She was growing into womanhood—just the sweet, closed bud of womanhood as yet—still a girl with the soft velvet of girlhood in her eyes, yet with the mystery of woman stirring gently in her soul, as if the Great Hand were hesitating between awakening her and letting her sleep a little longer. At these times, when the opportunity came to steal hours by herself, she would put on the red dress and do up her wonderful hair as she saw it in the pictures of the magazines Pierrot had sent up twice a year from Nelson House.

On the second day of Pierrot's absence Nepeese dressed herself like this, but today she let her hair cascade in a shining glory about her, and about her forehead bound a circlet of red ribbon. She was not yet done. Today she had marvelous designs. On the wall close to her mirror she had tacked a large page from a woman's magazine, and on this page was a lovely vision of curls. Fifteen hundred miles north of the sunny California studio in which the picture had been taken, Nepeese, with pouted red lips and puckered forehead, was fighting to master the mystery of the other girl's curls!

She was looking into her mirror, her face flushed and her eyes aglow in the exitement of the struggle to fashion one of the coveted ringlets from a tress that fell away below her hips, when the door opened behind her, and Bush McTaggart walked in.

CHAPTER XX

THE Willow's back was toward the door when the Factor from Lac Bain entered the cabin, and for a few startled seconds she did not turn. Her first thought was of Pierrot—for some reason he had returned. But even as this thought came to her, she heard in Baree's throat a snarl that brought her suddenly to her feet, facing the door.

McTaggart had not entered unprepared. He had left his pack, his gun, and his heavy coat outside. He was standing with his back against the door; and at Nepeese—in her wonderful dress and flowing hair—he was staring as if stunned for a space at what he saw. Fate, or accident, was playing against the Willow now. If there had been a spark of slumbering chivalry, of mercy, even, in Bush McTaggart's soul, it was extinguished by what he saw. Never had Nepeese looked more beautiful, not even on that day when MacDonald the mapmaker had taken her picture. The sun, flooding through the window, lighted up her marvelous hair; her flushed face was framed in its lustrous darkness like a tinted cameo. He had dreamed, but he had pictured nothing like this woman who stood before him now, her eyes widening with fear and the flush leaving her face even as he looked at her.

It was not a long interval in which their eyes met in that terrible silence—terrible to the girl. Words were unnecessary. At last she understood—understood what her peril had been that day at the edge of the chasm and in the forest, when fearlessly she had played with the menace that was confronting her now.

A breath that was like a sob broke from her lips.

"*M'sieu!*" She tried to say. But it was only a gasp—an effort. She seemed choking.

Plainly she heard the click of the iron bolt as it locked the door. McTaggart advanced a step.

Only a single step McTaggart advanced. On the floor

160

Baree had remained like a carven thing. He had not moved. He had not made a sound but that one warning snarl—until McTaggart took the step. And then, like a flash, he was up and in front of Nepeese, every hair of his body on end; and at the fury in his growl McTaggart lunged back against the barred door. A word from Nepeese in that moment, and it would have been over. But an instant was lost—an instant before her cry came. In that moment man's hand and brain worked swifter than brute understanding; and as Baree launched himself at the Factor's throat, there came a flash and a deafening explosion almost in the Willow's eyes.

It was a chance shot, a shot from the hip with McTaggart's automatic. Baree fell short. He struck the floor with a thud and rolled against the log wall. There was not a kick or a quiver left in his body. McTaggart laughed nervously as he shoved his pistol back in its holster. He knew that only a brain shot could have done that.

With her back against the farther wall, Nepeese was waiting. McTaggart could hear her panting breath. He advanced halfway to her.

"Nepeese, I have come to make you my wife." he said.

She did not answer. He could see that her breath was choking her. She raised a hand to her throat. He took two more steps, and stopped. He had never seen such eyes.

"I have come to make you my wife, Nepeese. To-morrow you will go on to Nelson House with me, and then back to Lac Bain—forever." He added the last word as an afterthought. "Forever," he repeated.

He did not mince words. His courage and his determination rose as he saw her body droop a little against the wall. She was powerless. There was no escape. Pierrot was gone. Baree was dead.

He had thought that no living creature could move as swiftly as the Willow when his arms reached out for her. She made no sound as she darted under one of his outstretched arms. He made a lunge, a brutal grab, and his fingers caught a bit of hair. He heard the snap of it as she tore herself free and flew to the door. She had thrown back the bolt when he caught her and his arms closed about her. He dragged her back, and now she cried out—cried out in despair for Pierrot, for Baree, for some miracle of God that might save her.

And Nepeese fought. She twisted in his arms until she was facing him. She could no longer see. She was smothered in her hair. It covered her face and breast and body, suffocating her, entangling her hands and arms—and still she fought. In the struggle McTaggart stumbled over the body of Baree, and they went down. Nepeese was up fully five seconds ahead of the man. She could have reached the door. But again it was her hair. She paused to fling back the thick masses of it so that she could see, and McTaggart was at the door ahead of her.

He did not lock it again, but stood facing her. His face was scratched and bleeding. He was no longer a man but a devil. Nepeese was broken, panting—a low sobbing came with her breath. She bent down, and picked up a piece of firewood. McTaggart could see that her strength was almost gone.

She clutched the stick as he approached her again. But McTaggart had lost all thought of fear or caution. He sprang upon her like an animal. The stick of firewood fell. And again fate played against the girl. In her terror and hopelessness she had caught up the first stick her hand had touched—a light one. With her last strength she struck at McTaggart with it, and as it fell on his head, he staggered back. But it did not make him loose his hold.

Vainly she was fighting now, not to strike him or to escape, but to get her breath. She tried to cry out again, but this time no sound came from between her gasping lips.

Again he laughed, and as he laughed, he heard the door open. Was it the wind? He turned, still holding her in his arms.

In the open door stood Pierrot.

CHAPTER XXI

D URING that terrible space which followed an eternity of time rolled slowly through the little cabin on the Gray Loon—that eternity which lies somewhere between life and death and which is sometimes meted out to a human life in seconds instead of eons.

In those seconds Pierrot did not move from where he stood in the doorway. McTaggart, huddled over with the weight in his arms, and staring at Pierrot, did not move. But the Willow's eyes were opening. And a convulsive quiver ran through the body of Baree, where he lay near the wall. There was not the sound of a breath. And then, in that silence, a great gasping sob came from Nepeese.

Then Pierrot stirred to life. Like McTaggart, he had left his coat and mittens outside. He spoke, and his voice was not like Pierrot's. It was a strange voice.

"The great God has sent me back in time, *m'sieu*," he said. "I, too, traveled by way of the east, and saw your trail where it turned this way."

No, that was not like Pierrot's voice! A chill ran through McTaggart now, and slowly he let go of Nepeese. She fell to the floor. Slowly he straightened.

"Is it not true, *m'sieu*?" said Pierrot again. "I have come in time?"

What power was it—what great fear, perhaps, that made McTaggart nod his head, that made his thick lips form huskily the words, "Yes—in time." And yet it was not fear. It was something greater, something more all-powered than that. And Pierrot said, in that same strange voice:

"I thank the great God!"

The eyes of madman met the eyes of madman now. Between them was death. Both saw it. Both thought that they saw the direction in which its bony finger pointed. Both were certain. McTaggart's hand did not go to the pistol in his holster, and Pierrot did not touch the knife in his belt. When they came together, it was throat to throat—two beasts now, instead of one, for Pierrot had in him the fury and strength of the wolf, the cat, and the panther.

McTaggart was the bigger and heavier man, a giant in strength; yet in the face of Pierrot's fury he lurched back over the table and went down with a crash. Many times in his life he had fought, but he had never felt a grip at his throat like the grip of Pierrot's hands. They almost crushed the life from him at once. His neck snapped—a little more, and it would have broken. He struck out blindly from his back, and twisted himself to throw off the weight of the halfbreed's body. But Pierrot was fastened there, as Sekoosew the ermine had fastened itself at the jugular of the partridge, and Bush McTaggart's jaws slowly swung open, and his face began to turn from red to purple.

Cold air rushing through the door, Pierrot's voice and the sound of battle roused Nepeese quickly to consciousness and the power to raise herself from the floor. She had fallen near Baree, and as she lifted her head, her eyes rested for a moment on the dog before they went to the fighting men. Baree was alive! His body was twitching; his eyes were open; he made an effort to raise his head as she was looking at him.

Then she dragged herself to her knees and turned to the men, and Pierrot, even in the blood-red fury of his desire to kill, must have heard the sharp cry of joy that came from her when she saw that it was the Factor from Lac Bain who was underneath. With a tremendous effort she staggered to her feet, and for a few moments she stood swaying unsteadily as her brain and her body readjusted themselves. Even as she looked down upon the blackening face from which Pierrot's fingers were choking the life, Bush McTaggart's hand was groping blindly for his pistol. He found it. Unseen by Pierrot, he dragged it from its holster. It was one of the black devils of chance that favored him again, for in his excitement he had not snapped the safety shut after shooting Baree. Now he had only strength left to pull the trigger. Twice his forefinger closed. Twice there came deadened explosion close to Pierrot's body.

In Pierrot's face Nepeese saw what had happened. Her heart died in her breast as she looked upon the swift and terrible change wrought by sudden death. Slowly Pierrot straightened. His eyes were wide for a moment—wide and sta̶ ̶ ̶ ̶ ̶ He made no sound. She could not see his lips m̶ ̶ ̶ ̶ And then he fell toward her, so that McTaggart's body was free. Blindly and with an agony that gave no evidence in cry or word she flung herself down beside him. He was dead.

How long Nepeese lay there, how long she waited

for Pierrot to move, to open his eyes, to breathe, she would never know. In that time McTaggart rose to his feet and stood leaning against the wall, the pistol in his hand, his brain clearing itself as he saw his final triumph. His work did not frighten him. Even in that tragic moment as he stood against the wall, his defense—if it ever came to a defense—framed itself in his mind. Pierrot had murderously assaulted him—without cause. In self-defense he had killed him. Was he not the Factor of Lac Bain? Would not the company and the law believe his word before that of this girl? His brain leaped with the old exultation. It would never come to that—to a betrayal of this struggle and death in the cabin—after he had finished with her! She would not be known for all time as *La Bête Noire*. No, they would bury Pierrot, and she would return to Lac Bain with him. If she had been helpless before, she was ten times more helpless now. She would never tell of what had happened in the cabin.

He forgot the presence of death as he looked at her, bowed over her father so that her hair covered him like a silken shroud. He replaced the pistol in its holster and drew a deep breath into his lungs. He was still a little unsteady on his feet, but his face was again the face of a devil. He took a step, and it was then there came a sound to rouse the girl. In the shadow of the farther wall Baree had struggled to his haunches, and now he growled.

Slowly Nepeese lifted her head. A power which she could not resist drew her eyes up until she was looking into the face of Bush McTaggart. She had almost lost consciousness of his presence; her senses were cold and deadened—it was as if her own heart had stopped beating along with Pierrot's. What she saw in the Factor's face dragged her out of the numbness of her grief back to the abyss of her own peril. He was standing over her. In his face there was no pity, nothing of horror at what he had done—only an insane exultation as he looked—not at Pierrot's dead body, but at her. He put out a hand, and it rested on her head. She felt his thick fingers crumpling her hair, and his eyes blazed like embers of fire behind watery films. She struggled to rise, but with his hands at her hair he held her down.

"Great God!" she breathed.

She uttered no other words, no plea for mercy, no other sound but a dry, hopeless sob. In that moment neither of them heard or saw Baree. Twice in crossing the cabin his hindquarters had sagged to the floor. Now he was close to McTaggart. He wanted to give a single lunge to the man-brute's back and snap his thick neck as he would have broken a caribou bone. But he had no strength. He was still partially paralyzed from his foreshoulder back. But his jaws were like iron, and they closed savagely on McTaggart's leg.

With a yell of pain the Factor released his hold on the Willow, and she staggered to her feet. For a precious half-minute she was free, and as the Factor kicked and struck to loose Baree's hold, she ran to the cabin door and out into the day. The cold air struck her face; it filled her lungs with new strength; and

168

without thought of where hope might lie she ran through the snow into the forest.

McTaggart appeared at the door just in time to see her disappear. His leg was torn where Baree had fastened his fangs, but he felt no pain as he ran in pursuit of the girl. She could not go far. An exultant cry, inhuman as the cry of a beast, came in a great breath from his gaping mouth as he saw that she was staggering weakly as she fled. He was halfway to the edge of the forest when Baree dragged himself over the threshold. His jaws were bleeding where McTaggart had kicked him again and again before his fangs gave way. Halfway between his ears was a seared spot, as if a red-hot poker had been laid there for an instant. This was where McTaggart's bullet had gone. A quarter of an inch deeper, and it would have meant death. As it was, it had been like the blow of a heavy club, paralyzing his senses and sending him limp and unconscious against the wall. He could move on his feet now without falling, and slowly he followed in the tracks of the man and the girl.

As she ran, Nepeese's mind became all at once clear and reasoning. She turned into the narrow trail over which McTaggart had followed her once before, but just before reaching the chasm, she swung sharply to the right. She could see McTaggart. He was not running fast, but was gaining steadily, as if enjoying the sight of her helplessness, as he had enjoyed it in another way on that other day. Two hundred yards below the deep pool into which she had pushed the Factor—

just beyond the shallows out of which he had dragged himself to safety—was the beginning of Blue Feather's Gorge. An appalling thing was shaping itself in her mind as she ran to it—a thing that with each gasping breath she drew became more and more a great and glorious hope. At last she reached it and looked down. And as she looked, there whispered up out of her soul and trembled on her lips the swan song of her mother's people:

> Our fathers—come!
> Come from out of the valley.
> Guide us—for today we die,
> And the winds whisper of death!

She had raised her arms. Against the white wilderness beyond the chasm she stood tall and slim. Fifty yards behind her the Factor from Lac Bain stopped suddenly in his tracks. "Ah," he mumbled. "Is she not wonderful!" And behind McTaggart, coming faster and faster, was Baree.

Again the Willow looked down. She was at the edge, for she had no fear in this hour. Many times she had clung to Pierrot's hand as she looked over. Down there no one could fall and live. Fifty feet below her the water which never froze was smashing itself into froth among the rocks. It was deep and black and terrible, for between the narrow rock walls the sun did not reach it. The roar of it filled the Willow's ears.

She turned and faced McTaggart.

Even then he did not guess, but came toward her

again, his arms stretched out ahead of him. Fifty yards!
It was not much, and shortening swiftly.

Once more the Willow's lips moved. After all, it is
the mother-soul that gives us faith to meet eternity—
and it was to the spirit of her mother that the Willow
called in the hour of death. With the call on her lips
she plunged into the abyss, her wind-whipped hair
clinging to her in a glistening shroud.

CHAPTER XXII

A MOMENT later the Factor from Lac Bain
stood at the edge of the chasm. His voice had
called out in a hoarse bellow—a wild cry of
disbelief and horror that had formed the Willow's name
as she disappeared. He looked down, clutching his
huge red hands and staring in ghastly suspense at the
boiling water and black rocks far below. There was
nothing there now—no sign of her, no last flash of her
pale face and streaming hair in the white foam. And
she had done *that*—to save herself from him!

The soul of the man-beast turned sick within him,
so sick that he staggered back, his vision blinded and
his legs tottering under him. He had killed Pierrot, and
it had been a triumph; all his life he had played the
part of the brute with a stoicism and cruelty that had
known no shock—nothing like this that overwhelmed

171

him now, numbing him to the marrow of his bones until he stood like one paralyzed. He did not see Baree. He did not hear the dog's whining cries at the edge of the chasm. For a few moments the world turned black for him; and then, dragging himself out of his stupor, he ran frantically along the edge of the gorge, looking down wherever his eyes could reach the water, striving for a glimpse of her. At last it grew too deep. There was no hope. She was gone—and she had faced *that* to escape him!

He mumbled that fact over and over again, stupidly, thickly, as though his brain could grasp nothing beyond it. She was dead. And Pierrot was dead. And he, in a few minutes, had accomplished it all.

He turned back toward the cabin—not by the trail over which he had pursued Nepeese, but straight through the thick bush. Great flakes of snow had begun to fall. He looked at the sky, where banks of dark clouds were rolling up from the south and east. The sun went out. Soon there would be a storm—a heavy snowstorm. The big flakes falling on his naked hands and face set his mind to work. It was lucky for him, this storm. It would cover everything—the fresh trails, even the grave he would dig for Pierrot.

It does not take such a man as the Factor long to recover from a moral concussion. By the time he came in sight of the cabin his mind was again at work on physical things—on the necessities of the situation. The appalling thing, after all, was not that both Pierrot and Nepeese were dead, but that his dream was shattered. It was not that Nepeese was dead, but that he had lost her. This was his vital disappointment. The other thing—his crime—it was easy to cover.

It was not sentiment that made him dig Pierrot's grave close to the princess-mother's under the tall spruce. It was not sentiment that made him dig the grave at all, but caution. He buried Pierrot decently. Then he poured Pierrot's stock of kerosene where it would be most effective and touched a match to it. He stood in the edge of the forest until the cabin was a mass of flames. The snow was falling thickly. The freshly made grave was a white mound, and the trails were filling. For the physical things he had done there was no fear in Bush McTaggart's heart as he turned back toward Lac Bain. No one would ever look into the grave of Pierrot du Quesne. And there was no one to betray him if such a miracle happened. But of one thing his black soul would never be able to free itself. Always he would see the pale, triumphant face of the Willow as she stood facing him in that moment of her glory when, even as she was choosing death rather than him, he had cried to himself: "Ah! Is she not wonderful!"

As Bush McTaggart had forgotten Baree, so Baree had forgotten the Factor from Lac Bain. When McTaggart had run along the edge of the chasm, Baree had squatted himself in the foot-beaten plot of snow where Nepeese had last stood, his body stiffened and his forefeet braced as he looked down. He had seen her take the leap. Many times that summer he had followed her in her daring dives into the deep, quiet water of the pool. But this was a tremendous distance.

173

She had never dived into a place like that. He could see the black heads of the rocks, appearing and disappearing in the whirling foam like the heads of monsters at play; the roar of the water filled him with dread; his eyes caught the swift rush of crumbled ice between the rock walls. And she had gone down there!

He had a great desire to follow her, to jump in, as he had always jumped in after her. She was surely down there, even though he could not see her. Probably she was playing among the rocks and hiding herself in the white froth and wondering why he didn't come. But he hesitated—hesitated with his head and neck over the abyss, and his forefeet giving way a little in the snow. With an effort he dragged himself back and whined. He caught the fresh scent of McTaggart's moccasins in the snow, and the whine changed slowly into a long snarl. He looked over again. Still he could not see her. He barked—the short, sharp signal with which he always called her. There was no answer. Again and again he barked, and always there was nothing but the roar of the water that came back to him. Then for a few moments he stood back, silent and listening, his body shivering with the strange dread that was possessing him.

The snow was falling now, and McTaggart had returned to the cabin. After a little Baree followed in the trail he had made along the edge of the chasm, and wherever McTaggart had stopped to peer over, Baree paused also. For a space his hatred of the man was burned up in his desire to join the Willow, and he continued along the gorge until, a quarter of a mile beyond where the Factor had last looked into it, he came to the narrow trail down which he and Nepeese had many times adventured in quest of rock violets. The twisting path that led down the face of the cliff was filled with snow now, but Baree cleared his way through it until at last he stood at the edge of the unfrozen torrent. Nepeese was not here. He whined, and barked again, but this time there was in his signal to her an uneasy repression, a whimpering note which told that he did not expect a reply. For five minutes after that he sat on his haunches in the snow, stolid as a rock. What it was that came down out of the dark mystery and tumult of the chasm to him, what spirit-whispers of nature that told him the truth, it is beyond the power of reason to explain. But he listened, and he looked; and his muscles twitched as the truth grew in him; and at last he raised his head slowly until his black muzzle pointed to the white storm in the sky, and out of his throat there went forth the quavering, long-drawn howl of the husky who mourns outside the tepee of a master who is newly dead.

On the trail, heading for Lac Bain, Bush McTaggart heard that cry and shivered.

It was the smell of smoke, thickening in the air until it stung his nostrils, that drew Baree at last away from the chasm and back to the cabin. There was not much left when he came to the clearing. Where the cabin had been was a red-hot, smoldering mass. For a long time he sat watching it, still waiting and still listening. He no longer felt the effect of the bullet that had stunned him, but his senses were undergoing another change now, as strange and unreal as their struggle against that darkness of near-death in the cabin. In a space that had not covered more than an hour the world had twisted itself grotesquely for Baree. That long ago the Willow was sitting before her little mirror in the cabin, talking to him and laughing in her happiness, while he lay in vast contentment on the floor. And now there was no cabin, no Nepeese, no Pierrot. Quietly he struggled to comprehend. It was some time before he moved from under the thick balsams, for already a deep and growing suspicion began to guide his movements. He did not go nearer to the smoldering mass of the cabin, but slinking low, made his way about the circle of the open to the dog corral. This took him under the tall spruce. For a full minute he paused here, sniffing at the freshly made mound under its white mantle of snow. When he went on, he slunk still lower, and his ears were flat against his head.

The dog corral was open and empty. McTaggart had seen to that. Again Baree squatted back on his haunches and sent forth the death howl. This time it was for Pierrot. In it there was a different note from that of the howl he had sent forth from the chasm: it was positive, certain. In the chasm his cry had been tempered with doubt—a questioning hope, something that was so almost human that McTaggart had shivered on the trail. But Baree *knew* what lay in that freshly dug snow-covered grave. A scant three feet of earth could not hide its secret from him. There was death—definite and unequivocal. But for Nepeese he was still hoping and seeking.

Until noon he did not go far from the cabin, but only once did he actually approach and sniff about the black pile of steaming timbers. Again and again he circled the edge of the clearing, keeping just within the bush and timber, sniffing the air and listening. Twice he went back to the chasm. Late in the afternoon there came to him a sudden impulse that carried him swiftly through the forest. He did not run openly now; caution, suspicion, and fear had roused in him afresh the instincts of the wolf. With his ears flattened against the side of his head, his tail drooping until the tip of it dragged the snow and his back sagging in the curious, evasive gait of the wolf, he scarcely made himself distinguishable from the shadows of the spruce and balsams.

There was no faltering in the trail Baree made; it was straight as a rope might have been drawn through the forest, and it brought him, early in the dusk, to the open spot where Nepeese had fled with him that day she had pushed McTaggart over the edge of the precipice into the pool. In the place of the balsam shelter of that day there was now a watertight birchbark tepee which Pierrot had helped the Willow to make during the summer. Baree went straight to it and thrust in his head with a low and expectant whine.

There was no answer. It was dark and cold in the tepee. He could make out indistinctly the two blankets that were always in it, the row of big tin boxes in which Nepeese kept their stores, and the stove which Pierrot had improvised out of scraps of iron and heavy tin. But Nepeese was not there. And there was no sign of her outside. The snow was unbroken except by his own trail. It was dark when he returned to the burned cabin. All that night he hung about the deserted dog corral, and all through the night the snow fell steadily, so that by dawn he sank into it to his shoulders when he moved out into the clearing.

But with day the sky had cleared. The sun came up, and the world was almost too dazzling for the eyes. It warmed Baree's blood with new hope and expectation. His brain struggled even more eagerly than yesterday to comprehend. Surely the Willow would be returning soon! He would hear her voice. She would appear suddenly out of the forest. He would receive some signal from her. One of these things, or all of them, *must* happen. He stopped sharply in his tracks at every sound, and sniffed the air from every point of the wind. He was traveling ceaselessly. His body made deep trails in the snow around and over the huge white mound where the cabin had stood; his tracks led from the corral to the tall spruce, and they were as numerous as the footprints of a wolf pack for half a mile up and down the chasm.

On the afternoon of this day the second big impulse came to him. It was not reason, and neither was it instinct alone. It was the struggle halfway between, the brute mind fighting at its best with the mystery of an intangible thing—something that could not be seen by the eye or heard by the ear. Nepeese was not in the cabin, because there was no cabin. She was not at the tepee. He could find no trace of her in the chasm. She was not with Pierrot under the big spruce.

Therefore, unreasoning but sure, he began to follow the old trapline into the north and west.

CHAPTER XXIII

NO man has ever looked clearly into the mystery of death as it is impinged upon the senses of the northern dog. It comes to him, sometimes, with the wind; most frequently it must come with the wind, and yet there are ten thousand masters in the Northland who will swear that their dogs have given warning of death hours before it actually came; and there are many of these thousands who know from experience that their teams will stop a quarter or half a mile from a stranger cabin in which there is unburied dead.

Yesterday Baree had smelled death, and he knew without process of reasoning that the dead was Pierrot. How he knew this, and why he accepted the fact as inevitable, is one of the mysteries which at times seems to give the direct challenge to those who concede nothing more than instinct to the brute mind. He knew that Pierrot was dead without exactly knowing what death was. But of one thing he was sure: he would never see Pierrot again; he would never hear his voice again; he would never hear again the *swish-swish-swish* of his snowshoes in the trail ahead, and so on the trapline he did not look for Pierrot. Pierrot was gone forever. But Baree had not yet associated death with Nepeese. He was filled with a great uneasiness; what came to him from out of the chasm had made him tremble with fear and suspense; he sensed the thrill of something strange, of something impending, and yet even as he had given the death howl in the chasm, it must have been for Pierrot. For he believed that Nepeese was alive, and he was now just as sure that he would overtake her on the trapline as he was positive yesterday that he would find her at the birch-bark tepee.

Since yesterday morning's breakfast with the Willow, Baree had gone without eating; to appease his hunger meant to hunt, and his mind was too filled with his quest of Nepeese for that. He would have gone hungry all that day, but in the third mile from the cabin he came to a trap in which there was a big snowshoe rabbit. The rabbit was still alive, and he killed it and ate his fill. Until dark he did not miss a trap. In one of them there was a lynx; in another a fisher cat; out on the white surface of a lake he sniffed at a snowy mound under which lay the body of a red fox killed by one of Pierrot's poison baits. Both the lynx and the fisher cat were alive, and the steel chains of their traps clanked sharply as they prepared to give Baree battle. But Baree was uninterested. He hurried on, his uneasiness growing as the day darkened and he found no sign of the Willow.

It was a wonderfully clear night after the storm—cold and brilliant, with the shadows standing out as clearly as living things. The third idea came to Baree now. He was, like all animals, largely of one idea at a time—a creature with whom all lesser impulses were governed by a single leading impulse. And this impulse, in the glow of the starlit night, was to reach as quickly as possible the first of Pierrot's two cabins on the trapline. There he would find Nepeese!

We won't call the process by which Baree came to this conclusion a process of reasoning; instinct or reasoning, whatever it was, a fixed and positive faith came to Baree just the same. He began to miss the traps in his haste to cover distance—to reach the cabin. It was twenty-five miles from Pierrot's burned home to the first trap cabin, and Baree had made ten of these by nightfall. The remaining fifteen were the most difficult. In the open spaces the snow was belly-deep and soft; frequently he plunged through drifts in which for a few moments he was buried. Three times during the early part of the night Baree heard the savage dirge of the wolves. Once it was a wild paean of triumph as the hunters pulled down their kill less than half a mile away in the deep forest. But the voice no longer called to him. It was repellent—a voice of hatred and of treachery. Each time that he heard it he stopped in his tracks and snarled, while his spine stiffened.

At midnight Baree came to the tiny amphitheater in the forest where Pierrot had cut the logs for the first of his trapline cabins. For at least a minute Baree stood at the edge of the clearing, his ears very alert, his eyes bright with hope and expectation, while he sniffed the air. There was no smoke, no sound, no light in the

181

one window of the log shack. His disappointment fell on him even as he stood there; again he sensed the fact of his aloneness, of the barrenness of his quest. There was a disheartened slouch to his body as he made his way through the snow to the cabin door. He had traveled twenty-five miles, and he was tired.

The snow was drifted deep at the doorway, and here Baree sat down and whined. It was no longer the anxious, questing whine of a few hours ago. Now it voiced hopelessness and a deep despair. For half an hour he sat shivering with his back to the door and his face to the starlit wilderness, as if there still remained the fleeting hope that Nepeese might follow after him over the trail. Then he burrowed himself a hole deep in the snowdrift and passed the remainder of the night in uneasy slumber.

With the first light of day Baree resumed the trail. He was not so alert this morning. There was the disconsolate droop to his tail which the Indians call the *Akoosewin*—the sign of the sick dog. And Baree was sick—not of body but of soul. The keenness of his hope had died, and he no longer expected to find the Willow. The second cabin at the far end of the trapline drew him on, but it inspired in him none of the enthusiasm with which he had hurried to the first. He traveled slowly and spasmodically, his suspicions of the forests again replacing the excitement of his quest. He approached each of Pierrot's traps and deadfalls cautiously, and twice he showed his fangs—once at a marten that snapped at him from under a root where it had dragged the trap in which it was caught, and the second time at a big snowy owl that had come to steal bait and was now a prisoner at the end of a steel chain. It may be that Baree thought it was Oohoom-isew and that he still remembered vividly the treach-erous assault and fierce battle of that night when, as a puppy, he was dragging his sore and wounded body through the mystery and fear of the big timber. For he did more than to show his fangs. He tore the owl into pieces.

There were plenty of rabbits in Pierrot's traps, and Baree did not go hungry. He reached the second trap-line cabin late in the afternoon, after ten hours of traveling. He met with no very great disappointment here, for he had not anticipated very much. The snow had banked this cabin even higher than the other. It lay three feet deep against the door, and the window was white with a thick coating of frost. At this place, which was close to the edge of a big barren, and un-sheltered by the thick forests farther back, Pierrot had built a shelter for his firewood, and in this shelter Baree made his temporary home. All the next day he re-mained somewhere near the end of the trapline, skirt-ing the edge of the barren and investigating the short side line of a dozen traps which Pierrot and Nepeese had strung through a swamp in which there had been many signs of lynx. It was the third day before he set out on his return to the Gray Loon.

He did not travel very fast, spending two days in covering the twenty-five miles between the first and the second trapline cabins. At the second cabin he remained for three days, and it was on the ninth day that he reached the Gray Loon. There was no change. There were no tracks in the snow but his own, made nine days ago.

Baree's quest for Nepeese became now more or less involuntary, a sort of daily routine. For a week he made his burrow in the dog corral, and at least twice between dawn and darkness he would go to the birchbark tepee and the chasm. His trail, soon beaten hard in the snow, became as fixed as Pierrot's trapline. It cut straight through the forest to the tepee, swinging slightly to the east so that it crossed the frozen surface of the Willow's swimming pool. From the tepee it swung in a circle through a part of the forest where Nepeese had frequently gathered armfuls of crimson fire-flowers, and then to the chasm. Up and down the edge of the gorge it went, down into the little cup at the bottom of the chasm, and thence straight back to the dog corral.

And then, of a sudden, Baree made a change. He spent a night in the tepee. After that, whenever he was at the Gray Loon, during the day he always slept in the tepee. The two blankets were his bed—and they were a part of Nepeese. And there, all through the long winter, he waited.

If Nepeese had returned in February and could have taken him unaware, she would have found a changed Baree. He was more than ever like a wolf; yet he never gave the wolf howl now, and always he snarled deep in his throat when he heard the cry of the pack. For several weeks the old trapline had supplied him with meat, but now he hunted. The tepee, in and out, was scattered with fur and bones. Once—alone—he caught a young deer in deep snow and killed it. Again, in the heart of a fierce February storm, he pursued a bull caribou so closely that it plunged over a cliff and broke its neck. He lived well, and in size and strength he was growing swiftly into a giant of his kind. In another six months he would be as large as Kazan, and his jaws were almost as powerful, even now.

Three times that winter Baree fought—once with a lynx that sprang down upon him from a windfall while he was eating a freshly killed rabbit, and twice with two lone wolves. The lynx tore him unmercifully before it fled into the windfall. The younger of the wolves he killed; the other fight was a draw. More and more he became an outcast, living alone with his dreams and his smoldering hopes.

And Baree did dream. Many times, as he lay in the tepee, he would hear the voice of Nepeese. He would hear her sweet calling, her laughter, the sound of his name, and often he would start up to his feet—the old Baree for a thrilling moment or two—only to lie down in his nest again with a low, grief-filled whine. And always when he heard the snap of a twig or some other sound in the forest, it was thought of Nepeese that flashed first into his brain. Someday she would return. That belief was a part of his existence as much as the sun and the moon and the stars.

The winter passed, and spring came, and still Baree continued to haunt his old trails, even going now and then over the old trapline as far as the first of the two cabins. The traps were rusted and sprung now; the thawing snow disclosed bones and feathers between their jaws; under the deadfalls were remnants of fur, and out on the ice of the lakes were picked skeletons of foxes and wolves that had taken the poison baits. The last snow went. The swollen streams sang in the forests and canyons. The grass turned green, and the first flowers came.

Surely this was the time for Nepeese to come home! He watched for her expectantly. He went still more frequently to their swimming pool in the forest, and he hung closely to the burned cabin and the dog corral. Twice he sprang into the pool and whined as he swam about, as though she surely must join him in their old water frolic. And now, as the spring passed and summer came, there settled upon him slowly the gloom and misery of utter hopelessness. The flowers were all out now, and even the *bakneesh* vines glowed like red fire in the woods. Patches of green were beginning to hide the charred heap where the cabin had stood, and the blueflower vines that covered the princess-mother's grave were reaching out toward Pierrot's, as if the princess-mother herself were the spirit of them.

All these things were happening, and the birds had mated and nested, and still Nepeese did not come! And at last something broke inside of Baree, his last hope, perhaps, his last dream; and one day he bade good-bye to the Gray Loon.

No one can say what it cost him to go; no one can say how he fought against the things that were holding him to the tepee, the old swimming pool, the familiar paths in the forest, and the two graves that were not so lonely now under the tall spruce. He went. He had no reason—simply went. It may be that there is a Master whose hand guides the beast as well as the man, and that we know just enough of this guidance to call it instinct. For, in dragging himself away, Baree faced the Great Adventure.

It was there, in the north, waiting for him—and into the north he went.

CHAPTER XXIV

IT was early in August when Baree left the Gray Loon. He had no objective in view. But there was still left upon his mind, like the delicate impression of light and shadow on a negative, the memories of his earlier days. Things and happenings that he had almost forgotten recurred to him now, as his trail led him farther and farther away from the Gray Loon; and his earlier experiences became real again, pictures thrown out afresh in his mind by the breaking of the last ties that held him to the home of the Willow. Involuntarily he followed the trail of these impressions—of these past happenings, and slowly they helped to build up new interests for him. A year in his life was a long time—a decade of man's experience. It was more than a year ago that he had left Kazan and Gray Wolf and the old windfall, and yet now there came back to him indistinct memories of those days of his earliest puppyhood, of the stream into which he had fallen, and of his fierce battle with Papayuchisew. It was his later experiences that roused the older memories. He came to the blind canyon up which Nepeese and Pierrot had chased him. That seemed but yesterday. He entered the little meadow, and stood beside the great rock that had almost crushed the life out of the Willow's body; and then he remembered where Wakayoo, his big bear friend, had died under Pierrot's rifle—and he smelled of Wakayoo's whitened bones where they lay scattered in the green grass, with flowers growing up among them. A day and night he spent in the little meadow before he went back out of the canyon and into his old haunts along the creek, where Wakayoo had fished for him. There was another bear here now, and he also was fishing. Perhaps he was a son or a grandson of Wakayoo. Baree smelled where he had made his fish caches, and for three days he lived on fish before he struck into the North.

And now, for the first time in many weeks, a bit of the old-time eagerness put speed into Baree's feet. Memories that had been hazy and indistinct through forgetfulness were becoming realities again, and as he would have returned to the Gray Loon had Nepeese been there so now, with something of the feeling of a wanderer going home, he returned to the old beaver pond.

It was that most glorious hour of a summer's day—sunset—when he reached it. He stopped a hundred yards away, with the pond still hidden from his sight, and sniffed the air, and listened. The *pond* was there. He caught the cool, honey smell of it. But Umisk, and Beaver-tooth, and all the others? Would he find them? He strained his ears to catch a familiar sound, and after a moment or two it came—a hollow splash in the water. He went quietly through the alders and stood at last close to the spot where he had first made the acquaintance of Umisk. The surface of the pond was undulating slightly; two or three heads popped up; he saw the torpedo-like wake of an old beaver towing a stick close to the opposite shore—he looked toward the dam, and it was as he had left it almost a year ago. He did not show himself for a time, but stood concealed in the young alders. He felt growing in him more and more a feeling of restfulness, a relaxation from the long strain of the lonely months during which he had waited for Nepeese. With a long breath he lay down among the alders, with his head just enough exposed to give him a clear view. As the sun settled lower the pond became alive. Out on the shore where he had saved Umisk from the fox came another generation of young beavers—three of them, fat and waddling. Very softly Baree whined.

All that night he lay in the alders. The beaver pond became his home again. Conditions were changed, of course, and as days grew into weeks the inhabitants of Beaver-tooth's colony showed no signs of accepting the grown-up Baree as they had accepted the baby Baree of long ago. He was big, black, and wolfish now—a long-fanged and formidable looking creature, and though he offered no violence he was regarded by the beavers with a deep-seated feeling of fear and suspicion. On the other hand, Baree no longer felt the old puppyish desire to play with the baby beavers, so their aloofness did not trouble him as in those other days. Umisk was grown up, too, a fat and prosperous young buck who was just taking unto himself this year a wife, and who was at present very busy gathering his winter's rations. It is entirely probable that he did not associate the big black beast he saw now and then with the little Baree with whom he had smelled noses once upon a time, and it is quite likely that Baree did not recognize Umisk except as a *part* of the memories that had remained with him.

All through the month of August Baree made the beaver pond his headquarters. At times his excursions kept him away for two or three days at a time. These journeys were always north, sometimes a little east and sometimes a little west, but never again into the south. And at last, early in September, he left the beaver pond for good.

For many days his wanderings carried him in no one particular direction. He followed the hunting, living chiefly on rabbits and that simple-minded species of partridge known as the "fool hen." This diet, of course, was given variety by other things as they happened to come his way. Wild currants and raspberries were ripening, and Baree was fond of these. He also liked the bitter berries of the mountain ash, which, along with the soft balsam and spruce pitch which he licked with his tongue now and then, were good medicine for him. In shallow water he occasionally caught a fish; now and then he hazarded a cautious battle with a porcupine, and if he was successful he feasted on the tenderest and most luscious of all the flesh that made up his menu. Twice in September he killed young deer. The big "burns" that he occasionally came to no longer held terrors for him; in the midst of plenty he forgot the days in which he had gone hungry. In October he wandered as far west as the Geikie River, and then northward to Wollaston Lake, which was a good hundred miles north of the Gray Loon. The first week in November he turned south again, following the Canoe River for a distance, and then swinging westward along a twisting creek called the Little Black Bear with No Tail. More than once during these weeks Baree came into touch with man, but, with the exception of the Cree hunter at the upper end of Wollaston Lake, no man had seen him. Three times in following the Geikie he lay crouched in the brush while canoes passed; half a dozen times, in the stillness of night, he nosed about cabins and tepees in which there was life, and once he came so near to the Hudson's Bay Company post at Wollaston that he could hear the barking of dogs and the shouting of their masters. And always he was seeking—questing for the thing that had gone out of his life. At the thresholds of the cabins he sniffed; outside of the tepees he circled close, gathering the wind; the canoes he watched with eyes in which there was a hopeful gleam. Once he thought the wind brought him the scent of Nepeese, and all at once his legs grew weak under his body and his heart seemed to stop beating. It was only for a moment or two. She came out of the tepee—an Indian girl with her hands full of willow-work—and Baree slunk away unseen.

It was almost December when Lerue, a halfbreed from Lac Bain, saw Baree's footprints in freshly fallen snow, and a little later caught a flash of him in the bush.

"*Mon Dieu*, I tell you his feet are as big as my hand, and he is as black as a raven's wing with the sun on it!" he exclaimed in the company's store at Lac Bain. "A fox? *Non!* He is half as big as a bear. A wolf—*oui!* And black as the devil, *M'sieus.*"

McTaggart was one of those who heard. He was putting his signature in ink to a letter he had written to the company when Lerue's words came to him. His hand stopped so suddenly that a drop of ink spattered on the letter. Through him there ran a curious shiver as he looked over at the halfbreed. Just then Marie came in. McTaggart had brought her back from her tribe. Her big, dark eyes had a sick look in them, and some of her wild beauty had gone since a year ago.

"He was gone like—that!" Lerue was saying, with a snap of his fingers. He saw Marie, and stopped.

"Black, you say?" McTaggart said carelessly, without lifting his eyes from his writing. "Did he not bear some dog mark?"

Lerue shrugged his shoulders.

"He was gone like the wind, *M'sieu.* But he was a wolf."

With scarcely a sound that the others could hear

Marie had whispered into the Factor's ear, and folding his letter McTaggart rose quickly and left the store. He was gone an hour. Lerue and the others were puzzled. It was not often that Marie came into the store; it was not often that they saw her at all. She remained hidden in the Factor's log house, and each time that he saw her Lerue thought that her face was a little thinner than the last, and her eyes bigger and hungrier-looking. In his own heart there was a great yearning. Many a night he passed the little window beyond which he knew that she was sleeping; often he looked to catch a glimpse of her pale face, and he lived in the one happiness of knowing that Marie understood, and that into her eyes there came for an instant a different light when their glances met. No one else knew. The secret lay between them—and patiently Lerue waited and watched. "Someday," he kept saying to himself— "someday"—and that was all. The one word carried a world of meaning and of hope. When that day came he would take Marie straight to the Missioner over at Fort Churchill, and they would be married. It was a dream—a dream that made the long days and the longer nights on the trapline patiently endured. Now they were both slaves to the environing Power. But— someday—

Lerue was thinking of this when McTaggart returned at the end of the hour. The Factor came straight up to where the half-dozen of them were seated about the big box stove, and with a grunt of satisfaction shook the freshly fallen snow from his shoulders.

"Pierre Eustach has accepted the Government's

offer, and is going to guide that mapmaking party up into the Barrens this winter," he announced. "You know, Lerue—he has a hundred and fifty traps and deadfalls set, and a big poison-bait country. A good line, eh? And I have leased it of him for the season. It will give me the outdoor work I need—three days on the trail, three days here. Eh, what do you say to the bargain?"

"It is good," said Lerue.

"Yes, it is good," said Roget.

"A wide fox country," said Mons Roule.

"And easy to travel," murmured Valence in a voice that was almost like a woman's.

CHAPTER XXV

THE trapline of Pierre Eustach ran thirty miles straight west of Lac Bain. It was not as long a line as Pierrot's had been, but it was like a main artery running through the heart of a rich fur country. It had belonged to Pierre Eustach's father, and his grandfather, and his great-grandfather, and beyond that it reached, Pierre averred, back to the very pulse of the finest blood in France. The books at McTaggart's post went back only as far as the great-grandfather end of it, the older evidence of ownership being at Churchill. It was the finest game country between Reindeer Lake and the Barren Lands. It was in December that Baree came to it.

Again he was traveling southward in a slow and wandering fashion, seeking food in the deep snows. The *Kistisew Kestin*, or Great Storm, had come earlier than usual this winter, and for a week after it, scarcely a hoof or claw was moving. Baree, unlike the other creatures, did not bury himself in the snow and wait for the skies to clear and crust to form. He was big, and powerful, and restless. Less than two years old, he weighed a good eighty pounds. His pads were broad and wolfish. His chest and shoulders were like a malamute's, heavy and yet muscled for speed. He was wider between the eyes than the wolf-breed husky, and his eyes were larger, and entirely clear of the *Wuttooi*, or blood film, that marks the wolf and also to an extent the husky. His jaws were like Kazan's, perhaps even more powerful. Through all that week of the Big Storm he traveled without food. There were four days of snow, with driving blizzards and fierce winds, and after that three days of intense cold in which every living creature kept to its warm dugout in the snow. Even the birds had burrowed themselves in. One might have walked on the backs of caribou and moose and not have guessed it. Baree sheltered himself during the worst of the storm but did not allow the snow to gather over him.

Every trapper from Hudson's Bay to the country of the Athabasca knew that after the Big Storm the famished fur animals would be seeking food, and that traps and deadfalls properly set and baited stood the biggest chance of the year of being filled. Some of them set out over their traplines on the sixth day; some on the seventh; and others on the eighth. It was on the seventh day that Bush McTaggart started over Pierre Eustach's line, which was now his own for the season. It took him two days to uncover the traps, dig the snow from them, rebuild the fallen "trap houses," and rearrange the baits. On the third day he was back at Lac Bain.

It was on this day that Baree came to the cabin at the far end of McTaggart's line. McTaggart's trail was fresh in the snow about the cabin, and the instant Baree sniffed of it every drop of blood in his body seemed to leap suddenly with a strange excitement. It took perhaps half a minute for the scent that filled his nostrils to associate itself with what had gone before, and at the end of that half-minute there rumbled in Baree's chest a deep and sullen growl. For many minutes after that he stood like a black rock in the snow, watching the cabin. Then slowly he began circling about it, drawing nearer and nearer, until at last he was sniffing at the threshold. No sound or smell of life came from inside, but he could smell the *old* smell of McTaggart. Then he faced the wilderness—the direction in which the trapline ran back to Lac Bain. He was trembling. His muscles twitched. He whined. Pictures were assembling more and more vividly in his mind—the fight in the cabin, Nepeese, the wild chase through the snow to the chasm's edge—even the memory of that age-old struggle when McTaggart had caught him in the rabbit snare. In his whine there was a great yearning, almost expectation. Then it died slowly away. After all, the scent in the snow was of a thing that he had hated and wanted to kill, and not of anything that he had loved. For an instant nature had impressed on him the significance of associations—a brief space only, and then it was gone. The whine died away, but in its place came again that ominous growl.

Slowly he followed the trail and a quarter of a mile from the cabin struck the first trap on the line. Hunger had caved in his sides until he was like a starved wolf. In the first trap house McTaggart had placed as bait the hindquarter of a snowshoe rabbit. Baree reached in cautiously. He had learned many things on Pierrot's line: he had learned what the snap of a trap meant; he had felt the cruel pain of steel jaws; he knew better than the shrewdest fox what a deadfall would do when the trigger was sprung—and Nepeese herself had taught him that he was never to touch a poison bait. So he closed his teeth gently in the rabbit flesh and drew it forth as cleverly as McTaggart himself could have done. He visited five traps before dark, and ate the five baits without springing a pan. The sixth was a deadfall. He circled about this until he had beaten a path in the snow. Then he went on into a warm balsam swamp and found himself a bed for the night.

The next day saw the beginning of the struggle that was to follow between the wits of man and beast. To Baree the encroachment of Bush McTaggart's trapline was not war; it was existence. It was to furnish him food, as Pierrot's line had furnished him food for many weeks. But he sensed the fact that in this instance he was lawbreaker and had an enemy to outwit. Had it been good hunting weather he might have gone on, for the unseen hand that was guiding his wanderings was drawing him slowly but surely back to the old beaver pond and the Gray Loon. As it was, with the snow deep and soft under him—so deep that in places he plunged into it over his ears—McTaggart's trapline was like a trail of manna made for his special use. He followed in the Factor's snowshoe tracks, and in the third trap killed a rabbit. When he had finished with it nothing but the hair and crimson patches of blood lay upon the snow. Starved for many days, he was filled with a wolfish hunger, and before the day was over he robbed the bait from a full dozen of McTaggart's traps. Three times he struck poison baits— venison or caribou fat in the heart of which was a dose of strychnine, and each time his keen nostrils detected the danger. Pierrot had more than once noted the amazing fact that Baree could sense the presence of poison even when it was most skillfully injected into the frozen carcass of a deer. Foxes and wolves ate of flesh from which his super-sensitive power of detecting the presence of deadly danger turned him away. So he passed Bush McTaggart's poisoned tidbits, sniffing them on the way, and leaving the story of his suspicion in the manner of his footprints in the snow. Where McTaggart had halted at midday to cook his dinner Baree made these same cautious circles with his feet.

The second day, being less hungry and more keenly alive to the hated smell of his enemy, Baree ate less

198

but was more destructive. McTaggart was not as skillful as Pierre Eustach in keeping the scent of his hands from the traps and "houses," and every now and then the smell of him was strong in Baree's nose. This wrought in Baree a swift and definite antagonism, a steadily increasing hatred where a few days before hatred was almost forgotten. There is, perhaps, in the animal mind a process of simple computation which does not quite achieve the distinction of reason, and which is not altogether instinct, but which produces results that might be ascribed to either. Baree did not add two and two together to make four; he did not go back step by step to prove to himself that the man to whom this trapline belonged was the cause of all his griefs and troubles—but he *did* find himself possessed of a deep and yearning hatred. McTaggart was the one creature except the wolves that he had ever hated; it was McTaggart who had hurt him, McTaggart who had hurt Pierrot, McTaggart who had made him lose his beloved Nepeese—*and McTaggart was here on this trapline!* If he had been wandering before, without object or destiny, he was given a mission now. It was to keep to the traps. To feed himself. And to vent his hatred and his vengeance as he lived.

The second day, in the center of a lake, he came upon the body of a wolf that had died of one of the poison baits. For a half-hour he mauled the dead beast until its skin was torn into ribbons. He did not taste the flesh. It was repugnant to him. It was his vengeance on the wolf breed. He stopped when he was half a dozen miles from Lac Bain, and turned back. At this particular point the line crossed a frozen stream beyond which was an open plain, and over that plain came—when the wind was right—the smoke and smell of the Post. The second night Baree lay with a full stomach in a thicket of banksian pine; the third day he was traveling westward over the trapline again.

Early on this morning Bush McTaggart started out to gather his catch, and where he crossed the stream six miles from Lac Bain he first saw Baree's tracks. He stopped to examine them with sudden and unusual interest, falling at last on his knees, whipping off the glove from his right hand, and picking up a single hair.

"The black wolf!"

He uttered the words in an odd, hard voice, and involuntarily his eyes turned straight in the direction of the Gray Loon. After that, even more carefully than before, he examined one of the clearly impressed tracks in the snow. When he rose to his feet there was in his face the look of one who had made an unpleasant discovery.

"A black wolf!" he repeated, and shrugged his shoulders. "Bah! Lerue is a fool. It is a dog." And then, after a moment, he muttered in a voice scarcely louder than a whisper, *"Her dog."*

He went on, traveling in the trail of the dog. A new excitement possessed him that was more thrilling than the excitement of the hunt. Being human, it was his privilege to add two and two together, and out of two and two he made—Baree. There was little doubt in his mind. The thought had flashed on him first when

Lerue had mentioned the black wolf. He was convinced after his examination of the tracks. They were the tracks of a dog, and the dog was black. Then he came to the first trap that had been robbed of its bait.

Under his breath he cursed. The bait was gone, and the trap was unsprung. The sharpened stick that had transfixed the bait was pulled out clean.

All that day Bush McTaggart followed a trail where Baree had left traces of his presence. Trap after trap he found robbed. On the lake he came upon the mangled wolf. From the first disturbing excitement of his discovery of Baree's presence his humor changed slowly to one of rage, and his rage increased as the day dragged out. He was not unacquainted with four-footed robbers of the trapline, but usually a wolf or a fox or a dog who had grown adept in thievery troubled only a few traps. But in this case Baree was traveling straight from trap to trap, and his footprints in the snow showed that he stopped at each. There was, to McTaggart, almost a human devilishness to his work. He evaded the poisons. Not once did he stretch his head or paw within the danger zone of a deadfall. For apparently no reason whatever he had destroyed a splendid mink, whose glossy fur lay scattered in worthless bits over the snow. Toward the end of the day McTaggart came to a deadfall in which a lynx had died. Baree had torn the silvery flank of the animal until the skin was of less than half value. McTaggart cursed aloud, and his breath came hot.

At dusk he reached the shack Pierre Eustach had built midway of his line, and took inventory of his fur.

It was not more than a third of a catch; the lynx was half ruined, a mink was torn completely in two. The second day he found still greater ruin, still more barren traps. He was like a madman. When he arrived at the second cabin, late in the afternoon, Baree's tracks were not an hour old in the snow. Three times during the night he heard the dog howling.

The third day McTaggart did not return to Lac Bain, but began a cautious hunt for Baree. An inch or two of fresh snow had fallen, and as if to take even greater measure of vengeance from his man-enemy Baree had left his footprints freely within a radius of a hundred yards of the cabin. It was half an hour before McTaggart could pick out the straight trail, and he followed this for two hours into a thick banksian swamp. Baree kept with the wind. Now and then he caught the scent of his pursuer; a dozen times he waited until the other was so close he could hear the snap of brush, or the metallic click of twigs against his rifle barrel. And then, with a sudden inspiration that brought the curses afresh to McTaggart's lips, he swung in a wide circle and cut straight back for the trapline. When the Factor reached the line, along toward noon, Baree had already begun his work. He had killed and eaten a rabbit; he had robbed three traps in the distance of a mile, and he was headed again straight over the trapline for Post Lac Bain.

It was the fifth day that Bush McTaggart returned to his post. He was in an ugly mood. Only Valence of the four Frenchmen was there, and it was Valence who heard his story, and afterward heard him cursing

202

Marie. She came into the store a little later, big-eyed and frightened, one of her cheeks flaming red where McTaggart had struck her. While the storekeeper was getting her the canned salmon McTaggart wanted for his dinner, Valence found the opportunity to whisper softly in her ear:

"*M'sieu* Lerue has trapped a silver fox," he said with low triumph. "He loves you, *mon amie*, and he will have a splendid catch by spring—and sends you this message from his cabin up on the Little Black Bear with No Tail: *Be ready to fly when the soft snows come!*"

Marie did not look at him, but she heard, and her eyes shone so like stars when the young storekeeper gave her the salmon that he said to Valence, when she had gone: "Blue Death, but she is still beautiful at times, Valence!"

To which Valence nodded with an odd smile.

CHAPTER XXVI

BY the middle of January the war between Baree and Bush McTaggart had become more than an incident—more than a passing adventure to the beast, and more than an irritating happening to the man. It was, for the time, the elemental *raison d'être* of their lives. Baree hung to the trapline.

He haunted it like a devastating specter, and each time that he sniffed afresh the scent of the Factor from Lac Bain he was impressed still more strongly with the instinct that he was avenging himself upon a deadly enemy. Again and again he outwitted McTaggart; he continued to strip his traps of their bait; the humor grew in him more strongly to destroy the fur he came across; his greatest pleasure came to be—not in eating—but in destroying. The fires of his hatred burned fiercer as the weeks passed, until at last he would snap and tear with his long fangs at the snow where McTaggart's feet had passed. And all of the time, away back of his madness, there was a vision of Nepeese that continued to grow more and more clearly in his brain. That first Great Loneliness—the loneliness of the long days and longer nights of his waiting and seeking on the Gray Loon, oppressed him again as it had oppressed him in the early days of her loss. On starry or moonlit nights he sent forth his wailing cries for her again, and Bush McTaggart, listening to them in the middle of the night, felt strange shivers run up his spine.

The man's hatred was different from the beast's, but perhaps even more implacable. With McTaggart it was not hatred alone. There was mixed with it an indefinable and superstitious fear, a thing he laughed at, a thing he cursed at, but which clung to him as surely as the scent of his trail clung to Baree's nose. Baree no longer stood for the animal alone; *he stood for Nepeese*. That was the thought that insisted in growing in McTaggart's ugly mind. Never a day passed now that he did not think of the Willow; never a night came and went without a visioning of her face. He even fancied, on a certain night of storm, that he heard her voice out in the wailing of the wind—and less than a minute later he heard faintly a distant howl out in the forest. That night his heart was filled with a leaden dread. He shook himself. He smoked his pipe until the cabin was blue. He cursed Baree, and the storm—but there was no longer in him the bullying courage of old. He had not ceased to hate Baree; he still hated him as he had never hated a man, but he had an even greater reason now for wanting to kill him. It came to him first in his sleep, in a restless dream, and after that it lived, and lived—*the thought that the spirit of Nepeese was guiding Baree in the ravaging of his trapline!*

After a time he ceased to talk at the Post about the Black Wolf that was robbing his line. The furs damaged by Baree's teeth he kept out of sight, and to himself he kept his secret. He learned every trick and scheme of the hunters who killed foxes and wolves along the Barrens. He tried three different poisons, one so powerful that a single drop of it meant death; he tried strychnine in gelatin capsules, in deer fat, caribou fat, moose liver, and even in the flesh of porcupine. At last, in preparing his poisons, he dipped his hands in beaver oil before he handled the venoms and flesh so that there could be no human smell. Foxes, wolves, and even the mink and ermine died of these baits, but Baree came always so near—and no nearer. In January McTaggart poisoned every bait in his trap-houses. This produced at least one good result for him. From that day Baree no longer touched his baits, but ate only the rabbits he killed in the traps.

It was in January that McTaggart caught his first glimpse of Baree. He had placed his rifle against a tree, and was a dozen feet away from it at the time. It was as if Baree knew, and had come to taunt him; for when the Factor suddenly looked up Baree was standing out clear from the dwarf spruce not twenty yards away from him, his white fangs gleaming and his eyes burning like coals. For a space McTaggart stared as if turned into stone. It was Baree. He recognized the white star, the white-tipped ear, and his heart thumped like a hammer in his breast. Very slowly he began to creep toward his rifle. His hand was reaching for it when like a flash Baree was gone.

This gave McTaggart his new idea. He blazed himself a fresh trail through the forests parallel with his trapline but at least five hundred yards distant from it. Wherever a trap or deadfall was set, this new trail struck sharply in, like the point of a V, so that he could approach his line unobserved. By this strategy he believed that in time he was sure of getting a shot at the dog. Again it was the man who was reasoning, and again it was the man who was defeated. The first day that McTaggart followed his new trail Baree also struck that trail. For a little while it puzzled him. Three times he cut back and forth between the old and the new trail. Then there was no doubt. The new trail was the *fresh* trail, and he followed in the footsteps of the Factor from Lac Bain. McTaggart did not know what was happening until his return trip, when he saw the story told in the snow. Baree had visited each trap, and without exception he had approached each time at the point of the inverted V. After a week of futile hunting, of lying in wait, of approaching at every point of the wind—a period during which McTaggart had twenty times cursed himself into fits of madness, another idea came to him. It was like an inspiration, and so simple that it seemed almost inconceivable that he had not thought of it before.

He hurried back to Post Lac Bain.

The second day after, he was on the trail at dawn. This time he carried a pack in which there were a dozen strong wolf traps freshly dipped in beaver oil, and a rabbit which he had snared the previous night. Now and then he looked anxiously at the sky. It was clear until late in the afternoon, when banks of dark clouds began rolling up from the east. Half an hour later a few flakes of snow began falling. McTaggart let one of these drop on the back of his mittened hand, and examined it closely. It was soft and downy, and he gave vent to his satisfaction. It was what he wanted. Before morning there would be six inches of freshly fallen snow covering the trails.

He stopped at the next traphouse and quickly set to work. First he threw away the poisoned bait in the "house" and replaced it with the rabbit. Then he began setting his wolf traps. Three of these he placed close to the "door" of the house, through which Baree would have to reach for the bait. The remaining nine he scattered at intervals of a foot or sixteen inches apart, so that when he was done a veritable cordon of traps guarded the house. He did not fasten the chains, but let them lay loose in the snow. If Baree got into one trap he would get into others and there would be no use of toggles. His work done, McTaggart hurried on through the thickening twilight of winter night to his shack. He was highly elated. This time there could be no such thing as failure. He had sprung every trap on his way from Lac Bain. In none of those traps would Baree find anything to eat until he came to the "nest" of twelve wolf traps.

Seven inches of snow fell that night, and the whole world seemed turned into a wonderful white robe. Like billows of feathers the snow hung to the trees and shrubs; it gave tall white caps to the rocks, and underfoot it was so light that a cartridge dropped from the hand sank to the bottom of it. Baree was on the trapline early. He was more cautious this morning, for there was no longer the scent or snowshoe track of McTaggart to guide him. He struck the first trap about halfway between Lac Bain and the shack in which the Factor was waiting. It was sprung, and there was no bait. Trap after trap he visited, and all of them he found sprung, and all without bait. He sniffed the air suspiciously, striving vainly to catch the tang of smoke, a whiff of the man-smell. Along toward noon he came to the "nest"—the twelve treacherous traps waiting for him with gaping jaws half a foot under the blanket of snow. For a full minute he stood well outside the danger line, sniffing the air, and listening. He saw the rabbit, and his jaws closed with a hungry click. He moved a step nearer. Still he was suspicious—for some strange and inexplicable reason he sensed danger. Anxiously he sought for it with his nose, his eyes, and his ears. And all about him there was a great silence and a great peace. His jaws clicked again. He whined softly. What was it stirring him? Where was the danger he could neither see nor smell? Slowly he circled about the traphouse; three times he circled round it, each circle drawing him a little nearer—until at last his feet almost touched the outer cordon of traps. Another minute he stood still; his ears flattened; in spite of the rich aroma of the rabbit in his nostrils *something was drawing him away*. In another moment he would have gone, but there came suddenly—and from directly behind the traphouse—a fierce little rat-like squeak, and the next instant Baree saw an ermine whiter than the snow tearing hungrily at the flesh of the rabbit. He forgot his strange premonition of danger. He growled fiercely, but his plucky little rival did not budge from his feast.

And then he sprang straight into the "nest" that Bush McTaggart had made for him.

CHAPTER XXVII

THE next morning Bush McTaggart heard the clanking of a chain when he was still a good quarter of a mile from the "nest." Was it a lynx? Was it a fisher cat? Was it a wolf or a fox? *Or was it Baree?* He half ran the rest of the distance, and at last he came to where he could see, and his heart leaped into his throat when he saw that he had caught his enemy. He approached, holding his rifle ready to fire if by any chance the dog should free himself.

Baree lay on his side, panting from exhaustion and quivering with pain. A hoarse cry of exultation burst from McTaggart's lips as he drew nearer and looked at the snow. It was packed hard for many feet about the traphouse, where Baree had struggled, and it was red with blood. The blood had come mostly from Baree's jaws. They were dripping now as he glared at his enemy. The steel jaws hidden under the snow had done their merciless work well. One of his forefeet was caught well up toward the first joint; both hind feet were caught; a fourth trap had closed on his flank, and in tearing the jaws loose he had pulled off a patch of skin half as big as McTaggart's hand. The snow told the story of his desperate fight all through the night; his bleeding jaws showed how vainly he had tried to break the imprisoning steel with his teeth. He was panting. His eyes were bloodshot. But even now, after all his hours of agony, neither his spirit nor his courage were broken. When he saw McTaggart he made a lunge to his feet, almost instantly crumpling down into the snow again. But his forefeet were braced. His head and chest remained up, and the snarl that came from his throat was tigrish in its ferocity. Here, at last—not more than a dozen feet from him— was the one thing in all the world that he hated more than he hated the wolf breed. And again he was helpless, as he had been helpless that other time in the rabbit snare.

The fierceness of his snarl did not disturb Bush McTaggart now. He saw how utterly the other was at his mercy, and with an exultant laugh he leaned his rifle against a tree, pulled off his mittens, and began loading his pipe. This was the triumph he had looked forward to, the torture he had waited for. In his soul there was a hatred as deadly as Baree's, the hatred that a man might have for a man. He had expected to send a bullet through the dog. But this was better— to watch him dying by inches, to taunt him as he would have taunted a human, to walk about him so that he could hear the clank of the traps and see the fresh blood drip as Baree twisted his tortured legs and body to keep facing him. It was a splendid vengeance. He was so engrossed in it that he did not hear the approach of snowshoes behind him. It was a voice—a man's voice—that turned him round suddenly.

The man was a stranger, and he was younger than McTaggart by ten years. At least he looked no more than thirty-five or -six, even with the short growth of blond beard he wore. He was of that sort that the average man would like at a glance; boyish, and yet a man; with clear eyes that looked out frankly from under the rim of his fur cap, a form lithe as an Indian's, and a face altogether that did not bear the hard lines of the wilderness. Yet McTaggart knew before he had spoken that this man *was* of the wilderness, that he was heart and soul a part of it. His cap was of fisher skin. He wore a windproof coat of softly tanned caribou skin, belted at the waist with a long sash, and Indian-fringed. The inside of the coat was furred. He was traveling on the long, slender bush-country snowshoe; his pack, strapped over the shoulders, was small and compact; he was carrying his rifle in a cloth jacket. And from cap to snowshoes he was *travel-worn*. McTaggart, at a guess, would have said that he had traveled a thousand miles in the last few weeks. It was not this thought that sent the strange and chilling thrill up his back, but the sudden fear that in some strange way a whisper of the truth might have found its way down into the south—the truth of what had happened on the Gray Loon—and that this travel-worn stranger wore under his caribou-skin coat the badge of the Royal Northwest Mounted Police. For that instant it was almost a terror that possessed him, and he stood mute.

The stranger had uttered only an amazed excla-mation before. Now he said, with his eyes on Baree: "God save us, but you've got the poor devil in a right proper mess, haven't you?"

There was something in the voice that reassured McTaggart. It was not a suspicious voice, and he saw that the stranger was more interested in the captured animal than in himself. He drew a deep breath.

"A trap robber," he said.

The stranger was staring still more closely at Baree. He thrust his gun stock downward in the snow and drew nearer to him.

"God save us again—a dog!" he exclaimed.

From behind, McTaggart was watching the man with the eyes of a ferret.

"Yes, a dog," he answered. "A wild dog, half wolf at least. He's robbed me of a thousand dollars' worth of fur this winter."

The stranger squatted himself before Baree, with his mittened hands resting on his knees, and his white teeth gleaming in a half-smile.

"You poor devil!" he said sympathetically. "So you're a trap robber, eh? An outlaw? And—the Police have got you! And—God save us once more—they haven't played you a very square game!"

He rose and faced McTaggart.

"I had to set a lot of traps like that," the Factor apologized, his face reddening slightly under the steady gaze of the stranger's blue eyes. Suddenly his animus rose. "And he's going to die there, inch by inch. I'm going to let him starve, and rot in the traps, to pay for all he's done." He picked up his gun, and added, with his eyes on the stranger and his finger ready at the trigger, "I'm Bush McTaggart, the Factor at Lac Bain. Are you bound that way, *M'sieu*?"

"A few miles. I'm bound up-country—beyond the Barrens."

McTaggart felt again the strange thrill.

"Government?" he asked.

The stranger nodded.

"The—Police, perhaps," persisted McTaggart.

"Why, yes—of course—the Police," said the stranger, looking straight into the Factor's eyes. "And now, *M'sieu*, as a very great courtesy to the Law I'm going to ask you to send a bullet through that beast's head before we go on. Will you? Or shall I?"

"It's the law of the line," said McTaggart, "to let a trap robber rot in the traps. And that beast was a devil. Listen—"

Swiftly, and yet leaving out none of the fine detail, he told of the weeks and months of strife between himself and Baree; of the maddening futility of all his tricks and schemes and the still more maddening cleverness of the beast he had at last succeeded in trapping.

"He was a devil—that clever," he cried fiercely when he had finished. "And now—would you shoot him, or let him lie there and die by inches, as the devil should?"

The stranger was looking at Baree. His face was turned away from McTaggart. He said:

"I guess you are right. Let the devil rot. If you're heading for Lac Bain, *M'sieu*, I'll travel a short distance with you now. It will take a couple of miles to straighten out the line of my compass."

He picked up his gun. McTaggart led the way. At the end of half an hour the stranger stopped, and pointed north.

"Straight up there—a good five hundred miles," he said, speaking as lightly as though he would reach home that night. "I'll leave you here."

He made no offer to shake hands. But in going, he said, "You might report that John Madison has passed this way."

After that he traveled straight northward for half a mile through the deep forest. Then he swung westward for two miles, turned at a sharp angle into the south, and an hour after he had left McTaggart he was once more squatted on his heels almost within arms' reach of Baree.

And he was saying, as though speaking to a human companion:

"So that's what you've been, old boy. A trap robber, eh? An *outlaw*? And you beat him at the game for two months! And for that, because you're a better beast than he is, he wants to let you die here as slow as you can. An *outlaw*!" His voice broke into a pleasant laugh, the sort of laugh that warms one, even a beast. "That's funny. We ought to shake hands. Boy, by George, we had! You're a wild one, he says. Well, so am I. Told him my name was John Madison. It ain't. I'm Jim Carvel. And, oh Lord!—all I said was 'Police.' And that was right. It ain't a lie. I'm wanted by the whole corporation—by every danged policeman between Hudson's Bay and the Mackenzie River. Shake, old man. We're in the same boat, an' I'm glad to meet you!"

CHAPTER XXVIII

JIM Carvel held out his hand, and the snarl that was in Baree's throat died away. The man rose to his feet. He stood there, looking in the direction taken by Bush McTaggart, and chuckled in a curious, exultant sort of way. There was friendliness even in that chuckle. There was friendliness in his eyes and in the shine of his teeth as he looked again at Baree. About him there was something that seemed to make the gray day brighter, that seemed to warm the chill air—a strange something that radiated cheer and hope and comradeship just as a hot stove sends out the glow of heat. Baree felt it. For the first time since the two men had come his trap-torn body lost its tenseness; his back sagged; his teeth clicked as he shivered in his agony. To *this* man he betrayed his weakness. In his bloodshot eyes there was a hungering look as he watched Carvel—the self-confessed outlaw. And Jim Carvel again held out his hand—much nearer this time.

"You poor devil," he said, the smile going out of his face. "You poor devil!"

The words were like a caress to Baree—the first he had known since the loss of Nepeese and Pierrot. He dropped his head until his jaw lay flat in the snow. Carvel could see the blood dripping slowly from it.

"You poor devil!" he repeated.

There was no fear in the way he put forth his hand. It was the confidence of a great sincerity and a great compassion. It touched Baree's head and patted it in a brotherly fashion, and then—slowly and with a bit more caution—it went to the trap fastened to Baree's forepaw. In his half-crazed brain Baree was fighting to understand things, and the truth came finally when he felt the steel jaws of the trap open, and he drew forth his maimed foot. He did then what he had done to no other creature but Nepeese. Just once his hot tongue shot out and licked Carvel's hand. The man laughed. With his powerful hands he opened the other traps, and Baree was free.

For a few moments he lay without moving, his eyes fixed on the man. Carvel had seated himself on the snow-covered end of a birch log and was filling his pipe. Baree watched him light it; he noted with new interest the first purplish cloud of smoke that left Carvel's mouth. The man was not more than the length of two trap chains away—and he grinned at Baree.

"Screw up your nerve, old chap," he encouraged. "No bones broke. Just a little stiff. Mebby we'd better—get out."

He turned his face in the direction of Lac Bain. The suspicion was in his mind that McTaggart might turn back. Perhaps that same suspicion was impressed upon Baree, for when Carvel looked at him again he was on his feet, staggering a bit as he gained his equilibrium. In another moment the outlaw had swung the packsack from his shoulders and was opening it. He thrust in his hand and drew out a chunk of raw, red meat.

"Killed it this morning," he explained to Baree.

"Yearling bull, tender as partridge—and that's as fine a sweetbread as ever came out from under a backbone. Try it!"

He tossed the flesh to Baree. There was no equivocation in the manner of its acceptance. Baree was famished—and the meat was flung to him by a friend. He buried his teeth in it. His jaws crunched it. New fire leapt into his blood as he feasted, but not for an instant did his reddened eyes leave the other's face. Carvel replaced his pack. He rose to his feet, took up his rifle, slipped on his snowshoes, and fronted the north.

"Come on, Boy," he said. "We've got to travel."

It was a matter-of-fact invitation, as though the two had been traveling companions for a long time. It was, perhaps, not only an invitation but partly a command. It puzzled Baree. For a full half-minute he stood motionless in his tracks gazing at Carvel as he strode into the north. A sudden convulsive twitching shot through Baree; he swung his head toward Lac Bain; he looked again at Carvel, and a whine that was scarcely more than a breath came out of his throat. The man was just about to disappear into the thick spruce. He paused, and looked back.

"Coming, Boy?"

Even at that distance Baree could see him grinning affably; he saw the outstretched hand, and the voice stirred new sensations in him. It was not like Pierrot's voice. He had never loved Pierrot. Neither was it soft and sweet like the Willow's. He had known only a few men, and all of them he had regarded with distrust.

But this was a voice that disarmed him. It was lureful in its appeal. He wanted to answer it. He was filled with a desire, all at once, to follow close at the heels of this stranger. For the first time in his life a craving for the friendship of man possessed him. He did not move until Jim Carvel entered the spruce. Then he followed.

That night they were camped in a dense growth of cedars and balsams ten miles north of Bush Mc-Taggart's trapline. For two hours it had snowed, and their trail was covered. It was still snowing, but not a flake of the white deluge sifted down through the thick canopy of boughs. Carvel had put up his small silk tent, and had built a fire; their supper was over, and Baree lay on his belly facing the outlaw, almost within reach of his hand. With his back to a tree Carvel was smoking luxuriously. He had thrown off his cap and his coat, and in the warm fireglow he looked almost boyishly young. But even in that glow his jaws lost none of their squareness, nor his eyes their clear alertness.

"Seems good to have someone to talk to," he was saying to Baree. "Someone who can understand, an' keep his mouth shut. Did you ever want to howl, an' didn't dare? Well, that's me. Sometimes I've been on the point of bustin' because I wanted to talk to someone, an' couldn't."

He rubbed his hands together, and held them out toward the fire. Baree watched his movements and listened intently to every sound that escaped his lips. His eyes had in them now a dumb sort of worship, a look that warmed Carvel's heart and did away with the vast loneliness and emptiness of the night. Baree had dragged himself nearer to the man's feet, and suddenly Carvel leaned over and patted his head.

"I'm a bad one, old chap," he chuckled. "You haven't got it on me—not a bit. Want to know what happened?" He waited a moment, and Baree looked at him steadily. Then Carvel went on, as if speaking to a human, "Let's see—it was five years ago, five years this December, just before Christmas time. Had a dad. Fine old chap, my dad was. No mother—just the dad, an' when you added us up we made just One. Understand? And along came a white-striped skunk named Hardy and shot him one day because Dad had worked against him in politics. Out an' out murder. An' they didn't hang that skunk! No, sir, they didn't hang him. He had too much money, an' too many friends in politics, an' they let 'im off with two years in the penitentiary. But he didn't get there. No—s'elp me God, he didn't get there!"

Carvel was twisting his hands until his knuckles cracked. An exultant smile lighted up his face, and his eyes flashed back the firelight. Baree drew a deep breath—a mere coincidence; but it was a tense moment for all that.

"No, he didn't get to the penitentiary," went on Carvel, looking straight at Baree again. "Yours truly knew what that meant, old chap. He'd have been pardoned inside a year. An' there was my dad, the biggest half of me, in his grave. So I just went up to that white-striped skunk right there before the Judge's eyes, an'

220

the lawyers' eyes, an' the eyes of all his dear relatives an' friends—*and I killed him!* And I got away. Was out through a window before they woke up, hit for the bush country, and have been eating up the trails ever since. An' I guess God was with me, Boy. For He did a queer thing to help me out summer before last, just when the Mounties were after me hardest an' it looked pretty black. Man was found drowned down in the Reindeer Country, right where they thought I was cornered; an' the good Lord made that man look so much like me that he was buried under my name. So I'm officially dead, old chap. I don't need to be afraid anymore so long as I don't get too familiar with people for a year or so longer, and 'way down inside me I've liked to believe God fixed it up in that way to help me out of a bad hole. What's *your* opinion? Eh?"

He leaned forward for an answer. Baree had listened. Perhaps, in a way, he had understood. But it was another sound than Carvel's voice that came to his ears now. With his head close to the ground he heard it quite distinctly. He whined, and the whine ended in a snarl so low that Carvel just caught the warning note in it. He straightened. He stood up then, and faced the south. Baree stood beside him, his legs tense and his spine bristling.

Afer a moment Carvel said: "Relatives of yours, old chap. Wolves."

He went into the tent for his rifle and cartridges.

CHAPTER XXIX

BAREE was on his feet, rigid as hewn rock, when Carvel came out of the tent, and for a few moments Carvel stood in silence, watching him closely. Would the dog respond to the call of the pack? Did he belong to them? Would he go—now? The wolves were drawing nearer. They were not circling, as a caribou or a deer would have circled, but were traveling straight—dead straight for their camp. The significance of this fact was easily understood by Carvel. All that afternoon Baree's feet had left a blood smell in their trail, and the wolves had struck the trail in the deep forest, where the falling snow had not covered it. Carvel was not alarmed. More than once in his five years of wandering between the Arctic and the Height of Land he had played the game with the wolves. Once he had almost lost, but that was out in the open Barren. Tonight he had a fire, and in the event of his firewood running out he had trees he could climb. His anxiety just now was centered in Baree. So he said, making his voice quite casual, "You aren't going, are you, old chap?"

If Baree heard him he gave no evidence of it. But Carvel, still watching him closely, saw that the hair along his spine had risen like a brush, and then he heard—growing slowly in Baree's throat—a snarl of ferocious hatred. It was the sort of snarl that had held back the Factor from Lac Bain, and Carvel, opening the breech of his gun to see that all was right, chuckled happily. Baree may have heard the chuckle. Perhaps it meant something to him, for he turned his head suddenly and with flattened ears looked at his companion.

The wolves were silent now. Carvel knew what that meant, and he was tensely alert. In the stillness the click of the safety on his rifle sounded with metallic sharpness. For many minutes they heard nothing but the crack of the fire. Suddenly Baree's muscles seemed to snap. He sprang back, and faced the quarter behind Carvel, his head level with his shoulders, his inch-long fangs gleaming as he snarled into the black caverns of the forest beyond the rim of firelight. Carvel had turned like a shot. It was almost frightening—what he saw. A pair of eyes burning with greenish fire, and then another pair, and after that so many of them that he could not have counted them. He gave a sudden gasp. They were like cat-eyes, only much larger. Some of them, catching the firelight fully, were red as coals, others flashed blue and green—living things without bodies. With a swift glance he took in the black circle of the forest. They were out there, too; they were on all sides of them, but where he had seen them first they were thickest. In these first few seconds he had forgotten Baree, awed almost to stupefaction by that monster-eyed cordon of death that hemmed them in. There were fifty—perhaps a hundred wolves out there, afraid of nothing in all this savage world but fire. They had come up without the sound of a padded foot or a broken twig. If it had been later, and they had been asleep, and the fire out—

He shuddered, and for a moment the thought got the better of his nerves. He had not intended to shoot except from necessity, but all at once his rifle came to his shoulder and he sent a stream of fire out where the eyes were thickest. Baree knew what the shots meant, and filled with the mad desire to get at the throat of one of his enemies he dashed in their direction. Carvel gave a startled yell as he went. He saw the flash of Baree's body, saw it swallowed up in the gloom, and in that same instant heard the deadly clash of fangs and the impact of bodies. A wild thrill shot through him. The dog had charged alone—and the wolves had waited. There could be but one end. His four-footed comrade had gone straight into the jaws of death!

He could hear the ravening snap of those jaws out in the darkness. It was sickening. His hand went to the Colt .45 at his belt, and he thrust his empty rifle butt downward into the snow. With the big automatic before his eyes he plunged out into the darkness, and from his lips there issued a wild yelling that could have been heard a mile away. With the yelling a steady stream of fire spat from the Colt into the mass of fighting beasts. There were eight shots in the automatic, and not until the plunger clicked with metallic emptiness did Carvel cease his yelling and retreat into the firelight. He listened, breathing deeply. He no longer saw eyes in the darkness, nor did he hear the movement of bodies. The suddenness and ferocity of his attack had driven back the wolf horde. But the dog! He caught his breath, and strained his eyes. A shadow was dragging itself into the circle of light. It was Baree. Carvel ran to him, put his arms under his shoulders, and brought him to the fire.

For a long time after that there was a questioning light in Carvel's eyes. He reloaded his guns, put fresh fuel on the fire, and from his pack dug out strips of cloth with which he bandaged three or four of the deepest cuts in Baree's legs. And a dozen times he asked, in a wondering sort of way,

"Now, what the deuce made you do that, old chap? What have *you* got against the wolves?"

All that night he did not sleep, but watched.

Their experience with the wolves broke down the last bit of uncertainty that might have existed between the man and the dog. For days after that, as they traveled slowly north and west, Carvel nursed Baree as he might have cared for a sick child. Because of the dog's hurts, he made only a few miles a day. Baree understood, and in him there grew stronger and stronger a great love for the man whose hands were as gentle as the Willow's and whose voice warmed him with the thrill of an immeasurable comradeship. He no longer feared him or had a suspicion of him. And Carvel, on his part, was observing things. The vast emptiness of the world about them, and their aloneness, gave him the opportunity of pondering over unimportant details, and he found himself each day watching Baree a little more closely. He made at last a discovery which interested him deeply. Always, when they halted on the trail, Baree would turn his face to the south; when they were in camp it was from the south that he nosed the wind most frequently. This was quite natural, Carvel thought, for his old hunting grounds were back there. But as the days passed he began to notice other things. Now and then, looking off into the far country from which they had come, Baree would whine softly, and on that day he would be filled with a great restlessness. He gave no evidence of wanting to leave Carvel, but more and more Carvel came to understand that some mysterious call was coming to him from out of the south.

It was the wanderer's intention to swing over into the country of the Great Slave, a good eight hundred miles to the north and west, before the mush snows came. From there, when the waters opened in springtime, he planned to travel by canoe westward to the Mackenzie and ultimately to the mountains of British Columbia. These plans were changed in February. They were caught in a great storm in the Wholdaia Lake country, and when their fortunes looked darkest Carvel stumbled on a cabin in the heart of a deep spruce forest, and in this cabin there was a dead man. He had been dead for many days, and was frozen stiff. Carvel chopped a hole in the earth and buried him.

The cabin was a treasure trove to Carvel and Baree, and especially to the man. It evidently possessed no other owner than the one who had died; it was comfortable and stocked with provisions; and more than that, its owner had made a splendid catch of fur before the frost bit his lungs and he died. Carvel went over them carefully and joyously. They were worth a thousand dollars at any post, and he could see no reason why they did not belong to him now. Within a week he had blazed out the dead man's snow-covered trapline and was trapping on his own account.

This was two hundred miles north and west of the Gray Loon, and soon Carvel observed that Baree did not face directly south in those moments when the strange call came to him, but south and east. And now, with each day that passed, the sun rose higher in the sky; it grew warmer; the snow softened underfoot, and in the air was the tremulous and growing throb of spring. With these things came the old yearning to Baree; the heart-thrilling call of the lonely graves back on the Gray Loon, of the burned cabin, the abandoned tepee beyond the pool—and of Nepeese. In his sleep he saw visions of things. He heard again the low, sweet voice of the Willow, felt the touch of her hand, was at play with her once more in the dark shades of the forest—and Carvel would sit and watch him as he dreamed, trying to read the meaning of what he saw and heard.

In April Carvel shouldered his furs up to the Hudson's Bay Company's post at Lac la Biche, which was still farther north. Baree accompanied him halfway, and then—at sundown Carvel returned to the cabin and found him there. He was so overjoyed that he caught the dog's head in his arms and hugged it. They lived in the cabin until May. The buds were swelling then, and the smell of growing things had begun to rise up out of the earth.

Then Carvel found the first of the early blueflowers. That night he packed up.

"It's time to travel," he announced to Baree. "And I've sort of changed my mind. We're going back— there."

And he pointed south.

CHAPTER XXX

A STRANGE humor possessed Carvel as he began the southward journey. He did not believe in omens, good or bad. Superstition had played a small part in his life, but h ssessed both curiosity and a love for adventure years of lonely wandering had developed in a wonderfully clear mental vision of things, which in other words might be called singularly active imagination. He knew that some irresistible force was drawing Baree back into the south—that it was pulling him not only along a given line of the compass, but to an exact point in that line. For no reason in particular the situation began to interest him more and more, and as his time was valueless, and he had no fixed destination in view, he began to experiment. For the first two days he marked the dog's course by compass. It was due south-east. On the third morning Carvel purposely struck a course straight west. He noted quickly the change in Baree—his restlessness at first, and after that the dejected manner in which he followed at his heels. Toward noon Carvel swung sharply to the south and east again, and almost immediately Baree regained his old eagerness, and ran ahead of his master.

After this, for many days, Carvel followed the trail of the dog.

"Mebby I'm an idiot, old chap," he apologized one evening. "But it's a bit of fun, after all—an' I've got to hit the line of rail before I can get over to the mountains, so what's the difference? I'm game—so long as you don't take me back to that chap at Lac Bain. Now—what the devil! Are you hitting for his trapline, to get even? If that's the case—"

He blew out a cloud of smoke from his pipe as he eyed Baree, and Baree, with his head between his forepaws, eyed him back.

A week later Baree answered Carvel's question by swinging westward to give a wide berth to Post Lac Bain. It was mid-afternoon when they crossed the trail along which Bush McTaggart's traps and deadfalls had been set. Baree did not even pause. He headed due south, traveling so fast that at times he was lost to Carvel's sight. A suppressed but intense excitement possessed him, and he whined whenever Carvel stopped to rest—always with his nose sniffing the wind out of the south. Springtime, the flowers, the earth turning green, the singing of birds, and the sweet breaths in the air were bringing him back to that great Yesterday when he had belonged to Nepeese. In his unreasoning mind there existed no longer a winter. The long months of cold and hunger were gone; in the new visionings that filled his brain they were forgotten. The birds and flowers and the blue skies had come back, and with them the Willow must surely have returned, and she was waiting for him now, just over there beyond that rim of green forest.

Something greater than mere curiosity began to take possession of Carvel. A whimsical humor became a fixed and deeper thought, an unreasoning anticipation that was accompanied by a certain thrill of subdued excitement. By the time they reached the old beaver pond the mystery of the strange adventure had a firm hold on him. From Beaver-tooth's colony Baree led him to the creek along which Wakayoo, the black bear, had fished, and thence straight to the Gray Loon.

It was early afternoon of a wonderful day. It was so still that the rippling waters of spring, singing in a thousand rills and streamlets, filled the forests with a droning music. In the warm sun the crimson *bakneesh* glowed like blood. In the open spaces the air was scented with the perfume of blueflowers. In the trees and bushes mated birds were building their nests. After the long sleep of winter, nature was at work in all her glory. It was *Unekepesim*, the Mating Moon, the Home Building Moon—and Baree was going home. Not to matehood—but to Nepeese. He knew that she was there now, perhaps at the very edge of the chasm where he had seen her last. They would be playing together again soon, as they had played yesterday, and the day before, and the day before that, and in his joy he barked up into Carvel's face, and urged him to greater speed. Then they came to the clearing, and once more Baree stood like a rock. Carvel saw the charred ruins of the burned cabin, and a moment later the two graves under the tall spruce. He began to understand as his eyes returned slowly to the waiting, listening dog. A great swelling rose in his throat, and after a moment or two he said softly, and with an effort, "Boy, I guess you're home."

Baree did not hear. With his head up and his nose tilted to the blue sky he was sniffing the air. What · it that came to him with the perfumes of the forests and the green meadow? Why was it that he trembled now as he stood there? What was there in the air? Carvel asked himself, and his questing eyes tried to answer the questions. Nothing. There was death here—death and desertion, that was all. And then, all at once, there came from Baree a strange cry—almost a human cry—and he was gone like the wind.

Carvel had thrown off his pack. He dropped his rifle beside it now, and followed Baree. He ran swiftly, straight across the open, into the dwarf balsams, and into a grass-grown path that had once been worn by the travel of feet. He ran until he was panting for breath, and then stopped, and listened. He could hear nothing of Baree. But that old worn trail led on under the forest trees, and he followed it.

Close to the deep, dark pool in which he and the Willow had disported so often Baree, too, had stopped. He could hear the rippling of water, and his eyes shone with a gleaming fire as he quested for Nepeese. He expected to see her there, her slim white body shimmering in some dark shadow of overhanging spruce, or gleaming suddenly white as snow in one of the warm plashes of sunlight. His eyes sought out their old hiding-places; the great split rock on the other side, the shelving banks under which they used to dive like otter, the spruce boughs that dipped down to the surface, and in the midst of which the Willow loved to screen her naked body while he searched the pool for her. And at last the realization was borne upon him that she was not there, that he had still farther to go.

He went on to the tepee. The little open space in which they had built their hidden wigwam was flooded with sunshine that came through a break in the forest to the west. The tepee was still there. It did not seem very much changed to Baree. And rising from the ground in front of the tepee was what had come to him faintly on the still air—the smoke of a small fire. Over that fire was bending a person, and it did not strike Baree as amazing, or at all unexpected, that this person should have two great shining braids down her back. He whined, and at his whine the person grew a little rigid, and turned slowly.

Even then it seemed quite the most natural thing in the world that it should be Nepeese, and none other. He had lost her yesterday. Today he had found her.

And in answer to his whine there came a sobbing cry straight out of the soul of the Willow.

Carvel found them there a few minutes later, the dog's head hugged close up against the Willow's breast, and the Willow was crying—crying like a little child, her face hidden from him on Baree's neck. He did not interrupt them, but waited; and as he waited something in the sobbing voice and the stillness of the forest seemed to whisper to him a bit of the story of the burned cabin and the two graves, and the meaning of the Call that had come to Baree from out of the south.

CHAPTER XXXI

THAT night there was a new campfire in the open. It was not a small fire, built with the fear that other eyes might see it, but a fire that sent its flames high. In the glow of it stood Carvel. And as the fire had changed from that small smoldering heap over which the Willow had cooked her dinner, so Carvel, the officially dead outlaw, had changed. The beard was gone from his face; he had thrown off his caribou-skin coat; his sleeves were rolled up to the elbows, and there was a wild flush in his face that was not altogether the tanning of wind

233

and sun and storm, and a glow in his eyes that had not been there for five years, perhaps never before. His eyes were on Nepeese. She sat in the firelight, leaning a little toward the blaze, her wonderful hair glowing warmly in the flash of it. Carvel did not move while she was in that attitude. He seemed scarcely to breathe. The glow in his eyes grew deeper—the worship of a man for a woman. Suddenly Nepeese turned and caught him before he could turn his gaze. There was nothing to hide in her own eyes. Like her face, they were flushed with a new hope and a new gladness. Carvel sat down beside her on the birch log, and in his hand he took one of her thick braids and crumpled it as he talked. At their feet, watching them, lay Baree.

"Tomorrow or the next day I am going to Lac Bain," he said, a hard and bitter note back of the gentle worship in his voice. "I will not come back until I have— killed him."

The Willow looked straight into the fire. For a time there was a silence broken only by the crackling of the flames, and in that silence Carvel's fingers weaved in and out of the silken strands of the Willow's hair. His thoughts flashed back. What a chance he had missed that day on Bush McTaggart's trapline—if he had only known! His jaws set hard as he saw in the red-hot heart of the fire the mental pictures of the day when the Factor from Lac Bain had killed Pierrot. She had told him the whole story. Her flight. Her plunge to what she had thought was certain death in the icy torrent of the chasm. Her miraculous escape from the

234

waters—and how she was discovered, nearly dead, by
Tuboa, the toothless old Cree whom Pierrot out of pity
had allowed to hunt in part of his domain. He felt
within himself the tragedy and the horror of the one
terrible hour in which the sun had gone out of the
world for the Willow, and in the flames he could see
faithful old Tuboa as he called on his last strength to
bear Nepeese over the long miles that lay between the
chasm and his cabin; he caught shifting visions of the
weeks that followed in that cabin, weeks of hunger
and of intense cold in which the Willow's life hung by
a single thread. And at last, when the snows were
deepest, Tuboa had died. Carvel's fingers clenched in
the strands of the Willow's braid. A deep breath rose
out of his chest, and he said, staring deep into the fire,
"Tomorrow I will go to Lac Bain."

For a moment Nepeese did not answer. She, too,
was looking into the fire. Then she said:

"Tuboa meant to kill him when the spring came,
and he could travel. When Tuboa died I knew that it
was I who must kill him. So I came, with Tuboa's gun.
It was fresh loaded—yesterday. And—*M'sieu Jeem*"—
she looked up at him, a triumphant glow in her eyes
as she added, almost in a whisper—"You will not go
to Lac Bain. *I have sent a messenger.*"

"A messenger?"

"Yes, Ookimow Jeem—a messenger. Two days ago.
I sent word that I had not died, but was here—waiting
for him—and that I would be *Iskwao* now, his wife.
Oo-oo, he will come, Ookimow Jeem—he will come
fast. And you shall not kill him. *Non!*" She smiled into

235

his face, and the throb of Carvel's heart was like a drum. "The gun is loaded," she said softly. "I will shoot."

"Two days ago," said Carvel. "And from Lac Bain it is—"

"He will be here tomorrow," Nepeese answered him. "Tomorrow, as the sun goes down, he will enter the clearing. I know. My blood has been singing it all day. Tomorrow—tomorrow—for he will travel fast, Ookimow Jeem. Yes, he will come fast."

Carvel had bent his head. The soft tresses gripped in his fingers were crushed to his lips. The Willow, looking again into the fire, did not see. But she *felt*— and her soul was beating like the wings of bird.

"Ookimow Jeem," she whispered—a breath, a flutter of the lips so soft that Carvel heard no sound.

If old Tuboa had been there that night it is possible he would have read strange warnings in the winds that whispered now and then softly in the treetops. It was such a night; a night when the Red Gods whisper low among themselves, a carnival of glory in which even the dipping shadows and the high stars seemed to quiver with the life of a potent language. It is barely possible that old Tuboa, with his ninety years behind him, would have learned something, or that at least he would have *suspected* a thing which Carvel in his youth and confidence did not see. Tomorrow—he will come tomorrow! The Willow, exultant, had said that. But to old Tuboa the trees might have whispered, *why not tonight?*

                    *   *   *

It was midnight when the big moon stood full above the little open in the forest. In the tepee the Willow was sleeping. In a balsam shadow back from the fire slept Baree, and still farther back in the edge of a spruce thicket slept Carvel. Dog and man were tired. They had traveled far and fast that day, and they heard no sound.

But they had traveled neither so far nor so fast as Bush McTaggart. Between sunrise and midnight he had come forty miles when he strode out into the clearing where Pierrot's cabin had stood. Twice from the edge of the forest he had called; and now, when he found no answer, he stood under the light of the moon and listened. Nepeese was to be here—waiting. He was tired, but exhaustion could not still the fire that burned in his blood. It had been blazing all day, and now—so near its realization and its triumph—the old passion was like a drunkening wine in his veins. Somewhere, near where he stood, Nepeese was waiting for him, *waiting for him*. Once again he called, his heart beating in a fierce anticipation as he listened. There was no answer. And then for a thrilling instant his breath stopped. He sniffed the air—and there came to him faintly the smell of smoke.

With the first instinct of the forest man he fronted the wind that was but a faint breath under the starlit skies. He did not call again, but hastened across the clearing. Nepeese was off there—somewhere—sleeping beside her fire, and out of him there rose a low

237

cry of exultation. He came to the edge of the forest; chance directed his steps to the overgrown trail; he followed it, and the smoke smell came stronger to his nostrils.

It was the forest man's instinct, too, that added the element of caution to his advance. That, and the utter stillness of the night. He broke no sticks under his feet. He disturbed the brush so quietly that it made no sound. When he came at last to the little open where Carvel's fire was still sending a spiral of spruce-scented smoke up into the air it was with a stealth that failed even to rouse Baree. Perhaps, deep down in him, there smoldered an old suspicion; perhaps it was because he wanted to come to her while she was sleeping. The sight of the tepee made his heart throb faster. It was light as day where it stood in the moonlight, and he saw hanging outside it a few bits of woman's apparel. He advanced soft-footed as a fox and stood a moment later with his hand on the cloth flap at the wigwam door, his head bent forward to catch the merest breath of sound. He could hear her breathing. For an instant his face turned so that the moonlight struck his eyes. They were aflame with a mad fire. Then, still very quietly, he drew aside the flap at the door.

It could not have been sound that roused Baree, hidden in the black balsam shadow a dozen paces away. Perhaps it was scent. His nostrils twitched first; then he awoke. For a few seconds his eyes glared at the bent figure in the tepee door. He knew that it was not Carvel. The old smell—the man-beast's smell, filled his nostrils like a hated poison. He sprang to his

238

feet and stood with his lips snarling back slowly from his long fangs. McTaggart had disappeared. From inside the tepee there came a sound; a sudden movement of bodies, a startled ejaculation of one awakening from sleep—and then a cry, a low, half-smothered, frightened cry, and in response to that cry Baree shot out from under the balsam with a sound in his throat that had in it the note of death.

In the edge of the spruce thicket Carvel rolled uneasily. Strange sounds were rousing him, cries that in his exhaustion came to him as if in a dream. At last he sat up, and then in sudden horror leaped to his feet and rushed toward the tepee. Nepeese was in the open, crying the name she had given him—"*Ookimow Jeem—Ookimow—Jeem—Ookimow—Jeem—*" She was standing there white and slim, her eyes with the blaze of the stars in them, and when she saw Carvel she flung out her arms to him, still crying:

"Ookimow Jeem—Oo-oo, Ookimow Jeem—"

In the tepee he heard the rage of a beast, the moaning cries of a man. He forgot that it was only last night he had come, and with a cry he swept the Willow to his breast, and the Willow's arms tightened round his neck as she moaned: "Ookimow Jeem—it is the man-beast—in there! It is the man-beast from Lac Bain—and Baree—"

Truth flashed upon Carvel, and he caught Nepeese up in his arms and ran away with her from the sounds that had grown sickening and horrible. In the spruce thicket he put her feet once more to the ground. Her arms were still tight around his neck; he felt the wild

239

terror of her body as it throbbed against him; her breath was sobbing, and her eyes were on his face. He drew her closer, and suddenly he crushed his face down close against hers and felt for an instant the warm thrill of her lips against his own. And he heard the whisper, soft and trembling.

"Ooo-oo, *Ookimow Jeem*—"

When Carvel returned to the fire, alone, his Colt in his hand, Baree was in front of the tepee waiting for him. Carvel picked up a burning brand and entered the wigwam. When he came out his face was white. He tossed the brand in the fire, and went back to Nepeese. He had wrapped her in his blankets, and now he knelt down beside her and put his arms around her.

"He is dead, Nepeese."

"Dead, Ookimow Jeem?"

"Yes. Baree killed him."

She did not seem to breathe. Gently, with his lips in her hair, Carvel whispered his plans for their paradise.

"No one will know, my sweetheart. Tonight I will bury him and burn the tepee. Tomorrow we will start for Nelson House, where there is a missioner. And after that—we will come back—and I will build a new cabin where the old one burned. *Do you love me, ka sakahet?*"

"*Oui*—yes—Ookimow Jeem—I love you—"

Suddenly there came an interruption. Baree at last was giving his cry of triumph. It rose to the stars; it wailed over the roofs of the forests and filled the quiet skies—a wolfish howl of exultation, of achievement, of vengeance fulfilled. Its echoes died slowly away, and silence came again. A great peace whispered in the soft breath of the treetops. Out of the north came the mating call of a loon. About Carvel's shoulders the Willow's arms crept closer. And Carvel, out of his heart, thanked God.

James Oliver Curwood, 1923, Mounds Resort, Houghton Lake, Michigan (Photo contributed with the kind permission of Ivan A. Conger, of Owosso, Michigan, editor of *The Curwood Collector*)

About the Author

JAMES OLIVER CURWOOD (1878–1927) was one of America's most popular wilderness adventure writers and an early conservationist, fighting for ecology long before it became the popular movement of today. He wrote thirty-three books, including *The Grizzly King,* the 1916 novel on which the movie *The Bear* is based, and which has been reissued by Newmarket Press under the title *The Bear: A Novel.* The character of James Langdon in this novel mirrors Curwood's own experience in the Canadian wilderness.

After serving as a newspaper reporter in Detroit, Curwood traveled throughout Canada, exploring its untainted beauty. He built his own log cabins from British Columbia to northern Quebec, often spending six months out of the year in the wilds of the North, and then would return to his hometown of Owosso, Michigan, to write about his adventures.

Curwood was a longtime hunter of wild game, but as he grew older—and especially after his experience of coming face to face with a grizzly who chose not to kill him—he favored the camera over a rifle because of his ever-increasing respect for animal life. Curwood fought to preserve the wilderness along with its inhabitants, which were being destroyed at an alarming rate at the turn of the century.

In 1927 he was appointed Chairman of the Game, Fish, and Wildlife Committee of the Michigan Department of Conservation. He became well known for his outspoken views on preserving the delicate balance of nature.

Curwood's other books, many of which were also made into films, include *The River's End* (which sold over 100,000 copies), *The Valley of Silent Men, God's Country: The Trail to Happiness, Nomads of the North, Kazan, The Flaming Forest,* and *The Gold Hunters*. His books have been translated into many languages, including Chinese.

Curwood has enjoyed tremendous popularity. *The New York Times Book Review* of February 1918 states: "Curwood has an invaluable gift of the born narrator—the ability to tell a story and tell it in an interesting and vivid way." During his lifetime Curwood enjoyed international fame for his novels and was regarded by many readers as being in a class with Jack London and Zane Grey.

Curwood is survived by a granddaughter and two great-grandchildren. His home is maintained as a historic site in Owosso, where a Curwood Festival is held annually. In 1979 a James Oliver Curwood Literary Award of Shiawassee County was established for the best essays written on the subjects of conservation and ecology.

NEWMARKET MEDALLION EDITIONS FOR YOUNG READERS

Ask for these titles at your local bookstore, or order from:
Newmarket Press, 18 East 48 Street, New York, NY 10017 (212) 832-3575

The Bear
James Oliver Curwood
The spectacular success of the movie triggered the rediscovery of this long-lost adventure story about Thor, a mighty grizzly, and Muskwa, a motherless bear cub, who travel from on adventure to another wile trappers draw nearer and nearer. "Spellbinding — as thrilling as the movie." — *The Kirkus Reviews*
(208 pp; 5³/₁₆" x 8")

Kazan, Father of Baree
James Oliver Curwood
The thrilling and truly unforgettable story of Kazan, three-quarters dog and one-quarter wolf, the mightiest canine of the Canadian wilderness.
(240 pp; 5³/₁₆" x 8")

Baree, The Story of a Wolf-Dog
James Oliver Curwood
The third book in Curwood's Nature Series is a powerful adventure story about a half-wild wolf pup separated from his parents in the Canadian wilderness, and the otters, rabbits, owls, bears, and other creatures he encounters there. "A timeless tale . . . Curwood captures the simplicity and beauty of nature." — *ALA Booklist*
(256 pp; 5³/₁₆" x 8")

The Totally Awesome Money Book for Kids (and Their Parents)
Adriane Berg and Arthur Berg Bochner
For young readers from ten to seventeen, this fun, fact-filled guide uses quizzes, games, riddles, forms, charts, stories, and drawings, to cover the basics of saving, investing, borrowing, working, and taxes. "Perfect for kids who want to know what they can do with their money."—*Newsday*
(160 pp; 5³/₁₆" x 8")

The Totally Awesome Business Book for Kids
Adriane Berg and Arthur Berg Bochner
This follow-up to the popular *The Totally Awesome Money Book for Kids (and Their Parents)* features information young people need to know about starting businesses, estimating profits and returns, and assessing steps needed to succeed. Includes sections on budgeting, record keeping, researching, organizing, marketing, negotiating, and working with others, even parents.
(160 pp; 5³/₁₆" x 8")

Street Fighter
Todd Strasser, based on the screenplay by Steven E. de Souza
The novelization—and only book—of the live-action film based on the phenomenally successful video game series, which brings to life all the fabulous characters already known to millions of kids from 5-15.
(160 pp; 5³/₁₆" x 8")

Fly Away Home
A novel by Patricia Hermes from the screenplay by Robert Rodat and Vince McKewin
A thrilling family adventure inspired by the true "Father Goose" story, starring Jeff Daniels and Anna Paquin, from the team who made *The Black Stallion* and *Never Cry Wolf.* Tie-in to Columbia Pictures film.
(160 pp + 8-pp color section; 5³/₁₆" x 8")

Dances With Wolves: The Illustrated Screenplay and Story Behind the Film
(see following page)

DANCES WITH WOLVES BOOKS FROM NEWMARKET PRESS

Dances With Wolves: The Illustrated Screenplay and Story Behind the Film
Kevin Costner, Michael Blake, and Jim Wilson
Here is the actual screenplay of the Academy Award-winning movie, 16 pages of
behind-the-scenes stories, and over 40 pictures and drawings.
(144 pp; 5 3/16" x 8")

Dances With Wolves: The Illustrated Story of the Epic Film
Kevin Costner, Michael Blake, and Jim Wilson. Photos by Ben Glass
The topselling illustrated moviebook of all time includes screenplay, production notes,
the complete credit roll, editorial and art features on Native Americans, the frontier, the
Civil War, and exclusive introductions by the authors.
(160 pp; 8 3/8" x 10 7/8"; 170 photos and drawings, 80 pages in color)

Dances With Wolves: A Story for Children
Adapted by James Howe, based on the Michael Blake screenplay.
For all ages—a children's version of the now classic story of John Dunbar's life on the
frontier among the Indians, illustrated with 68 color photos from the movie.
(64 pp; 8 3/8" x 10 7/8")

Dances With Wolves — The Novel
Michael Blake
The original novel that was the inspiration and basis for the award-winning movie, with
a new afterword by the author.
(336 pp; 5 1/2" x 8 1/4")

Order from your local bookstore or write to:
Newmarket Press, 18 East 48th Street, New York, NY 10017

Please send me:

____ *The Bear* @ $3.95(pb)

____ *The Bear* @ $16.95(hc)

____ *Kazan, Father of Baree* @ $4.50(pb)

____ *Baree, The Story of a Wolf-Dog* @ $3.95(pb)

____ *Baree, The Story of a Wolf-Dog* @ $18.95(hc)

____ *Totally Awesome Money Book for Kids* @ $10.95(pb)

____ *Totally Awesome Money Book for Kids* @ $18.95(hc)

____ *Totally Awesome Business Book for Kids* @ $10.95(pb)

____ *Street Fighter* @ $4.50(pb)

____ *Fly Away Home* @ $6.95(pb)

____ *Dances With Wolves: Illustrated Screenplay* @ $4.95(pb)

____ *Dances With Wolves: Illustrated Story* @ $16.95(pb)

____ *Dances With Wolves: Illustrated Story* @ $29.95(hc)

____ *Dances With Wolves: Story for Children* @ $14.95(hc)

____ *Dances With Wolves — The Novel* @ $18.95(hc)

For postage and handling, add $2.50 for the first book, plus $1.00 for each additional
book. Allow 4-6 weeks for delivery. Prices and availability are subject to change.

I enclose a check or money order for $_____ payable to Newmarket Press.

Name _____

Address _____

City/State/Zip _____

Special discounts are available for orders of five or more copies. For information, contact:
Newmarket Press, Special Sales Dept.• 18 East 48th Street, New York, NY 10017 • Tel: 212-
832-3575 or 800-669-3903; Fax: 212-832-3629